By the way, did I ever tell you ...

For Raphael Gygax, Rita Ackermann, Andro Wekua and all those who don't find it strange when an anteater sits down at the breakfast table.

jrp|ringier

ANNA   Did I ever tell you that it's always cold?

It's always really cold. Maybe we did have a summer once, but I've forgotten it. I think you always remember the nastier things in life. It's because they produce stronger feelings. And that can be proven. Let's think of something lovely, like a nice summer's day for example, when you're running around the place in a bunny costume and studying little animals. Perfectly normal, I do it all the time. Okay, I admit, I can't think of anything nice. Fine. So instead I'll talk about something awful: our unheated flat, the people in this town, the aliens in my class, the country I live in, the fact that I look pretty peculiar and that I can't talk to anyone. And so it goes on.

I have endless negative memories. They hang around in my stomach. I still remember every single one and how I felt; I'll never ever forget. Although that's probably rubbish, because if I start never forgetting now, in thirty years' time I'll consist of nothing but memories and there'll be no room in my head for anything else. Although I do think that's exactly what happens with old people, they're always telling stories about the 'olden days'. I just don't know how they can be so sure that they actually experienced all those memories. Perhaps at some stage they were on a spaceship and had a memory transplant. Extraterrestrial A: 'ensaqf. qvclamq' (which roughly translated means: Look, a couple of unsightly East Germans, let's transplant a few memories into them). Extraterrestrial B: 'fjhediqigheuijsabnb' (That's precisely what we'll do).

As you know, aliens are always in fashion.

I think I'm called Anna because old-fashioned names are always in fashion, just like aliens. It could have been much much worse. Many girls in my class are called Peggy, Mandy or Francise – and in our Thuringian dialect it comes out as – Fraenzeeese. Which hurts.

The town I live in is situated in the region of Thuringia. People here speak a kind of dialect that sounds like eating porridge. Parents in Thuringia, in fact parents in East Germany, give their poor children such extraordinary foreign names to reflect their incredible longing for the big wide world. I'll be 14 soon. Well, in a little while. Nearly a year to be exact. I don't know if I'm a normal 14-year old. I don't feel like a child any more. My terra is no longer as firma as it was when I was a child, I never really thought about such things then and so can't compare, as I have no idea how I used to feel.

There, I've lost my thread. That often happens. I'm thinking miles ahead and then my thoughts get too complicated for me.

Anyway, the town I live in is a small town. That's what it's called. I mean, I'd never have thought that up. You don't grow up one day and think: hey, can you believe it, this is one small town.

The only proper big city I know is Berlin. Berlin is a big deal. Anyway, that's enough of an introduction.

When I look around, this is what I see: I'm standing at the window in my room and looking down on a main road with the occasional Trabant or Wartburg* car driving up and down. They make muffled, lonely noises and puff vapour out into the cold. There really are only two makes of car, although occasionally a Skoda or a Wolga appears, but that's the lot. You don't just go into a shop and buy a car. You have to register and then ten years later, with a bit of luck, you get your car. That means that there is relatively little traffic on the road. A lorry drives past every three to five minutes.

Dustbins line the side of the road. In winter they smoulder away because people throw glowing embers into the rubbish and that sets everything else on fire. (Glowing embers are what's left after burning coal and wood. I'm writing this down in case these notes are not discovered by future generations until after my death.) That is why in winter there is always smog hanging over the town, not from the couple of cars, but from the factories and the smouldering rubbish. Although if I was looking out over the town from a well-heated flat it might well appear romantic. But this is not a warm flat.

I don't believe that anywhere else in the world can be as cold as it is here. Although I have to admit I don't know much about the rest of the world. I've got a few ideas, but I'll come back to those later.

It is so cold in my bedroom that when I breathe out my breath forms proper clouds. Not just puffs! Get the picture? There is a small iron stove but my mother has stupidly forgotten to order coal, and so the stove stays cold. Sometimes I burn stuff I find in the street, wood and whatnot. The stove glows for half an hour and then a few minutes later it seems colder than ever.

The flat is like this: one room with a wardrobe and junk in it and a window looking out onto the courtyard. It is not only cold, it is also dark and damp. Between you and me, I think that ghosts live in this room, well, as far as ghosts can live. They live in the wardrobe and are a family of dead farmers or workers. Sometimes I talk to them, 'Please, tell me, what was it really like building up the GDR with your bare hands?' And they reply, 'We did indeed build the anti-imperialistic defensive wall to protect our people and the achievements of socialism.' 'I see,' I say, and then I withdraw. There's no way you can have a proper conversation with people like that.

My mother's room is off a hallway that stinks of the freezing earth-closet (well, at least we have our own). Hers is cold too, and ever so slightly smoky. My mother smokes two to three packs of cigarettes a day. Does anyone understand grown-ups?

The bathtub is in the kitchen. Should anyone want a bath in ice-cold water, well, this is the perfect place. There is a kind of boiler that you heat up in order to take a bath, but then we're back to the old problem of the missing coal. To have a wash, you heat up water in a saucepan on the cooker (at least that is gas) and then pour it into a washbasin. This doesn't exactly encourage children to be clean. Washing is either cold or unpleasant, in either case it requires effort. I usually smile and manage without.

Despite all of the above, this apartment is a deluxe model. In the last flat the stove in the kitchen had to be heated with wood – and we never had any wood, as my mother always forgot to order that too. The bathtub stood in the cellar, and right next to it was a huge metal cauldron** to boil clothes in. (Future generations: I have heard that in the West you have washing machines, well we don't have them here. Here, clothes are thrown into cold water and boiled up, stirred with a huge wooden spoon and then hauled out and hung up in the garden still soaking wet. Or if you don't have a garden, then over the bath. Years later the washing is dry, stiff as a board and has the same old musty smell.) Of course, the cauldron was heated with wood. And water from this cauldron was used for the bath. Having a bath wasn't much fun either because once I got in, I never dared get out again. It was the cellar and it was cold. What's more there were spiders hanging around everywhere with long legs that wobbled. They should have drunk less.

So, what I want to say is that this flat really is luxurious. Most people I know ... okay, time to confess: I'm the not the sort of person who people really want to get to know. Or to be more precise: no-one wants to decorate their life with my friendship. I think that most people find me odd. I can't blame them – I think that I'm odd too. For example, I have a thing about finding it hard to follow my thoughts through. There are too many interesting side-roads off the main thought-road.

What I want to say is that in the East no-one lives particularly well. For most people the toilet is outside the flat in the passageway and several families share the cold earth-closet. (Note to future generations: an earth-closet is a toilet down which the stuff falls to the depths without being flushed down with water. It smells bad and a draught comes up from below.) There is no double-glazing. The apartment blocks are badly insulated. The plaster is crumbling, the roofs are leaky. And so on and so on. It's because everyone pays such little rent and because the apartment blocks belong to the state so no-one feels responsible for them.

Very few people live in newly built flats. I went to one once. It was totally amazing. The heating was the kind you simply switched on, and hot water came out of the taps. Unbelievable! It was like a hotel. Well, ok – it was how I imagined a hotel to be. I'm not really familiar with hotels. In fact, I'm not really familiar with anything out of the ordinary. Here, all the grown-ups look grey and overweight, and all the children are badly dressed.

I once read some newspapers and a catalogue from the West. Everything was so impossibly colourful you felt it must smell nice too. I studied it for hours and still couldn't believe that people could buy all that stuff. I know it's stupid, but I got the feeling I'd be as happy as a pig in poo with all those colourful things. We can only buy Western goods for Western money in Intershops. This is completely stupid. Officially the shops are only for tourists from the West. However the truth is that people often use Western money on the black market. For example: a builder will only put in a new washbasin for you if you pay him partly with Western money. The money comes from Western relatives and all sorts of other places – I've no idea where.

I go to the Intershop now and then. I can't describe how it smells: of soap and things that are foreign. And it has Lego and jeans. I get quite dizzy in the shop and very sad when I have to leave. Not because of the products but because of the weird and wonderful life that exists behind them. They have colour, while we only have black and white or, to be more accurate, a sort of grey.

It's actually quite odd that I notice all this because I don't know any better. But I see things quite clearly: my town is grey, and so is the whole country. People drag themselves through the streets and there's no place for them to go apart from their unheated flats with the crumbling plaster. So they sit there and I have absolutely no idea what they do. There are no lovely cafés or restaurants, no parks and no shopping centres. Some people have televisions: two channels in black and white. There's always something on about the heroic acts of the workers, or films about grey people sitting around in unheated flats. It's the same at the cinema: films from Russia about sad people in unheated flats – but with subtitles. Thanks a bunch.

This year there was a really good film: *Next Year on Lake Balaton*. It was great. A boy from the East met a girl from Holland while hitchhiking. They fell in love, you saw them naked, then she returned to Holland and he couldn't go with her because he was from the East. Hitchhiking would be a great thing to do.

The only other thing that helps is reading. But we are not allowed to read everything because it could spoil us. At least that's what the librarian said when I wanted to read *The Catcher in the Rye*. She is very old, with sensible brown shoes and a huge lump on her big toe. Once I even had a dream about her feet: they were travelling in boats. I asked her how words could spoil you. She replied that only words can do that and secretly gave me a copy of *Pippi Longstocking*. 'You could say this is also forbidden,' she said. I felt a bit dirty after reading the book. Who on earth believes in girls able to do magic? If it was true all the girls round here would be gone in a flash.

I've been reading since I was five. For the same reason that all book-hungry children read of course: to escape reality. But I ask you, how can you not want to run away from here? When I'm in the library encircled by books I feel happy and no longer alone. I get completely keyed up when I find a wonderful new book. That sounds very dull, but it's true.

* A model of car once popular in the GDR.

** These were huge metal containers built into a brick surround, and a fire was lit underneath to heat the water and boil the clothes.

MAX   Can you kill clocks?

The clock is ticking. Man, is there any noise more irritating than the ticking of a clock when everything else has shut up? ('As a clock, I must say that I'd imagined a more exciting existence than hanging around some boring boy's bedroom and ticking away. But hey – a clock's got to do what a clock's got to do!')

There's nothing to do at the moment because stupidly I finished clearing out my room last week. I woke up whenever and it was a Sunday like today. I didn't want to get up but with the best will in the world I couldn't find a reason to stay in bed. So I put my feet on the rug by my bed and looked at them. What the feet really wanted to do was run away. They stood on the dirty rug and studied the room. What a pigsty. Socks lying around on every surface and a smell of damp dog. That's when I thought to myself, there's no reason in hell why anyone should live in a room like this – and began to clear up. I got rid of ancient board games, along with cuddly toys and an old football that I'd never kicked because I loathe football, quite specifically because playing solo is not fun as it reminds you that no-one else wants to play with you. I thought that a tidy and clear room meant a tidy and clear mind. I hoped it would clear up my thoughts because I just have too many that end up in dead ends.

I'm perfectly normal, apart from the fact that I occasionally talk to objects or people I see in the street. In my head. For example, I might see the actress from *Next Year on Lake Balaton*. Occasionally I rehearse with her. I'll give you an example: if I catch the lights on green then I will definitely meet the actress. (She has freckles and is obviously older than me, probably much older. Even so, she would fall in love with me because I have tidied out my room.) However I've not actually met her yet.

My name is Maximilian. Evidently no-one can be bothered to say a name that long so they all call me Max, which I don't like. Maxes are usually fat. But who cares, I'm not exactly a person who is constantly being called. I live alone with my father. He hardly says a word. My mother is dead. Which is still no reason for people to drop their chins to the floor and mutter 'Oooh, I'm so very sorry,' as most do. Firstly because it's quite clear that they're not very sorry. Fair enough, they didn't know my mother. Secondly, I didn't know her either. She died when I was born. Well, shortly after. I only know her from a couple of photos. They show a woman laughing and wearing fairly adventurous clothes. I keep on getting out the photos and studying them to try and make myself feel something for the woman, but it's very difficult. Sometimes I think to myself things might be easier with a mother. Perhaps less gloomy. But I don't know if that's true or not.

I'd probably be less peculiar if I had a mother. But I only know my father, and if I'm not someone people like to call, then I'm certainly not someone people want to get to know.

ANNA   Did I ever tell you how rubbish Sundays are?

So, coming back to reality, it is Sunday. If I say I'm not a great fan of weekdays then I must add that I can't stand weekends. Everything appears to be dead at the weekend. What do I mean, APPEARS to be dead, it is dead. There was probably a nuclear bomb warning and once again I didn't cotton on.

Not that things are really buzzing during the week. The town I live in, hey, that sounds as if I had chosen it, no way, I just happen to live here, so, as I was saying, the town where I was born is not very big. You can walk from top to bottom and from left to right in just one hour. Although there's no reason why you should.

The highlights of the town are: an ice-cream parlour that makes fairly good ice cream even though I have to admit I have nothing to compare it with – it's the only ice cream parlour in town; a shop that sells roast chicken; a swimming pool open in summer – I went there a couple of times but don't go any more because I get the feeling that everyone's staring at me; and a park

I never go to on my own because gangs of youths hang out there, smoking, and I'm afraid of them.

There are only a few shops and they all sell the same crap: cheese (two varieties), cabbage (two varieties), apples (one variety), bread (a wheat/rye mix, always stale), butter, sausage (one variety) and jars of gherkins – so I'm talking about food shops here. The clothes in the shops that sell clothes are totally foul. And there are boring toys. It puts people in a bad mood when they buy that stuff. It leaves them feeling frustrated. How do I know this? Because everyone is always moaning and pouting and feeling betrayed. No idea by whom. People often feel that others are to blame if things aren't going well for them. And I have to say that includes me.

The socialist ideal is that everyone should have the same, that everyone feels okay and that all are equal. But I don't think that's how people work. If someone studies for six years to become a doctor then he wants to earn more money for his efforts so that he can afford more, otherwise he could just as easily do an apprenticeship, go to work in a factory and do a job that requires no thought. So there are a couple of glitches in the system.

Especially since 'everyone is equal' isn't true. Anyone who has been to the Baltic Sea or any other lake can see lots of old villas with boat launches that belong to people who are 'something to do with the Party'. (It is important to be in the SED – the only party in socialist Germany – if you want to do anything in life. All non-Party members are a little suspect. Our country is a country of workers and farmers, so animals are suspect, as are children, doctors and professors. I'm just mentioning this for future generations who might discover these notes.)

So that's how it is in the GDR. I have no idea what it's like anywhere else. Hanging over everything is the smell of winter and never-ending boredom. People just don't know what to do with themselves. Perhaps people in general don't have a clue, but I have a feeling that elsewhere, i.e. the countries that I'll never see, there'd be enough things to distract people from their boredom. Here the only thing adults can do to make something happen is drink a lot of alcohol. Or maybe they do that so they don't notice that nothing is happening.

Sadly that includes my mother, but more about her later.

As long as they are small, children can play normal children's games. They only begin to get bored when they go to school. This country is hell for young people. There is absolutely nothing for them to do apart from watch Russian films in the cinema or hang around the monument in town. But I don't even do that because I'm afraid of the others. Did I mention that?

I'm pretty much afraid of all sorts of things. When I'm with other people I seem to see myself from outside my body and then I just freeze. I can't think of anything to say and if I do, then I hear myself saying something that doesn't come from me. I really only relax when I'm reading. I've also got this watching thing. I have the feeling that everyone I meet is staring at me or laughing at me or despising me. But I suspect that's stupid because I'm certainly not important enough for everyone to stare at me or to have an opinion about me. One thing is sure, no-one out there is worrying about me.

MAX   On the subject of parents.

My father works with the police. That's mistake number one. If you're bragging about your parents' profession, then policeman is fairly nearly the bottom of the list – it's almost as bad as teacher.

He sort of looks how a father should look. I can never really tell with adults whether they're good looking or not and I don't much care anyway. I'm not even sure if adults have any feelings or not, they always appear so under control.

When my father comes home, he hangs up his uniform jacket and hat, locks his pistol away, then he clears his throat and we sit down at the table in silence. He eats whatever I've cooked, without saying a word, then he clears his throat again and sits down in front of the television and watches the latest heroic deeds of workers and farmers. That's right, we own a television. Because my father is with the police we have certain things that other people don't have. A telephone, for example. Hardly anyone else has a telephone so actually it's no big deal because there's no-one to phone up anyway.

Once my father has watched television and drunk his beer he goes off to bed. He always clears his throat beforehand and then stands there swaying for a few moments in the room. At weekends when he's not on duty he goes to football matches. Now and then he takes me with him – unfortunately. Football is deadly boring and the whole thing is not helped by having to meet my father's friends. They slap me on the back, talk nonsense and drink beer. 'Well, well, you really have grown, you'll soon be a proper man, come on, have a nip of beer, it'll make you grow quicker.' And: 'Have you got a girlfriend yet?' Wink wink, laugh, laugh, elbow in the ribs – my ribs. I don't know if it's the fate of all young boys to turn out like these men, but if there is another way then that is the way I'm going to go.

If I ask my father how he is, he says: 'Needs must.' I have a feeling he has no idea how he is. He simply doesn't ask himself the question. I watch my father very carefully and try to do everything differently. I read a lot, loathe sport and have no friends. I'll never drink beer, and I will never ever go on about the GDR being the best country in the world. How can anyone say that? It's true that everyone has an apartment and enough to eat. But surely there must be more to life. It can't all be so GREY.

The only thing I can hope for is that I grow up and go away. At some point I'm going to get out of this country, I know that for sure. But at the moment the only thing I have is a globe. I look at it and think out different routes for the boat. I'll moor up and visit countries. Samoa sounds good. I read a book about it once; it was printed in 1910 and had black and white photographs. The Samoans were all smiling, they were half-naked and had incredibly long hair. I have to admit that the half-naked business gave it an added boost. But if other boys don't like me, what chance have I got with girls?

I'm nearly fourteen. Why did I just think about girls in that context? It doesn't matter. I'm nearly fourteen and I've never had a friend. Okay, I know what you're thinking, in every class there's always a couple of idiotic prats who manage to find each other, but I can't even find a prat to get excited about me. I think this could be a real problem because I'm not exactly the type who goes up to people. Virtually never. I can never think of anything I could say to people. Or should say. If I absolutely force myself to talk to someone it's always a disaster. 'Hey, do you think there's still a danger of being buried alive to-day?' I ask that sort of thing sometimes because

I find it really interesting. The other boys in my class then look at me embarrassed, as if I'm mentally ill. For the other boys I'm a complete freak because I cook and shop and clean up, and because I ask stupid questions about being buried alive – for example.

So that's why I've stopped making an effort to talk. I do the housework, I read, and every year I learn something new. Not the stuff from school, but things that you really don't need. I study microbiology, everything about embalming, how to build zeppelins and that sort of thing. I'll be really educated by the time I'm thirty and so have a good chance of surviving when I leave this country. Then, if I get some sort of dull job working in a spare parts factory in Toronto, or sweeping up a bar in Samoa, at least I'll have my broad education and be able to occupy my mind with scientific questions while carrying out the tasks.

I'd really like to have a completely normal home, well, at least, how I imagine a completely normal home. That's why I cook and clean and put stupid tablecloths on the table. But I suspect that none of this really helps. It's quite obvious that I do not live in a normal household.

Sometimes I can barely stand the silence that radiates from my father. I asked him once if he missed my mother and if he was looking for another woman. I mean, it took a lot of nerve to ask but I really just wanted a conversation. I don't know what I was thinking of: that he'd flop down next to me on the sofa and we'd start to chat, and then he'd fetch a beer and we'd put on our pyjamas and carry on talking. Instead my father just cleared his throat and studied the television with renewed interest. He didn't say a thing. Absolutely not a thing. And I was left standing there in the doorway, my question like some old suitcase at my feet.

ANNA   Did I ever tell you about my mother?

I don't look like my mother on the inside or on the outside. She is small and has dark hair. Nor like my father. He is tall and has dark hair. I'm just different.

Sometimes I imagine what it would be like to be a child that had been swapped at birth. The idea of new parents is something I think about when nothing else works. It's my very best idea. I can build it up and expand it like a film. These parents enter my thoughts and each time they come from another interesting country. For example, I might make them Brazilians who own horses. But then sometimes the film doesn't come out as it should because I can't envisage what Brazil might be like, or Australia or Patagonia for that matter. But between you and me, has anyone got any idea what Patagonia is like? If they did, they'd certainly win first prize in the conjure-up-an-image competition (run by aliens, of course).

The country I fancy most is Holland. I imagine it to be fresh and clean, with seafarers, the wind steady at the rafters and plenty of cheese. Little old houses nestling next to little rivers, little smoke coming out of little chimneys and little songs coming out of the mouths of teenie-weenie Dutchmen. That's where my parents sometimes come from. The dream goes like this: I wave good-bye to my mother, she is a little sad because she has swapped me for a blonde Dutch youth she can't communicate with. My new parents, however, speak excellent German and we sail away in a boat. Don't pin me down on the details of getting to Holland by boat. The ship moors up and we live in a wonderful, old, well-heated house next to a river. My room is sunny and full of books — in German, of course. And Barbie dolls.

I must confess to a weakness: I would love to have a Barbie doll. I don't play with things really and I have not got a clue what I'd do with a Barbie doll, but hey, everyone has to have some quirk. By the way, my dreams never take place in West Germany. In my head it is really ugly. Like here, only more bleak. We were taught that all Nazis either came from the West, or disappeared back over there. Don't think I'm stupid enough to believe everything we're taught at school. I don't believe that the entire Federal Republic of Germany is full of junkies like Christiane F staggering around Bahnhof Zoo, or that everyone is unemployed, or that they are constantly killing each other. I do believe that there are Germans living in the Federal Republic. They're bound to be alright, just not the sort of people ideally suited to the adoption fantasies of a child. It might be that my parents come from Italy. Which leads me straight to Doges, even though I'm not quite sure who these Doges are, I really like the word. They sound like glorious hats. I once read about the Doges' Palace in a comic.

My parents, i.e. my fake parents who live here in the GDR, are divorced, but this is perfectly normal as nearly all parents here are divorced. In this country everyone marries very young, at 18, in order to get an apartment. Otherwise you don't get one. Some people have to share their flat with strangers. We lived with an old woman once. She'd sit in the kitchen from four o'clock in the morning and look out of the window. She smelt terrible, a sort of sour smell, and I have to say I was afraid of her.

But back to the young people. So they're given an apartment, mostly it's a two-room flat in an old building, and then by mistake they have children and become aware very quickly that they're in fact not grown-up enough to carry on like this for another fifty years. After that they all get very disappointed and want to be somewhere else with someone else.

In my case it's a bit more difficult than that. I'm not really anything yet. I don't really have any idea if anything will become of me or even what that anything might be. However there is no way of avoiding the fact that I must have a profession. Everyone works here. Most people don't care what they do as no-one earns a great deal more than anyone else. And if they did have more money, then there's nothing to spend it on. Exciting holidays abroad? You must be joking. The most you can hope for are holidays in sad hostels or private accommodation on Lake Balaton or in the Harz mountains, where you get a wood-lined room in an apartment along with a hotplate and a tea-strainer. For one hundred marks you can have a super jolly fortnight on your travels.

What else? You can't buy houses or things to wear. Everyone runs around in the same old stuff and lives in similarly rotting flats. There is simply no such thing as someone being unemployed and not able to afford chic holidays in rented rooms in somebody's flat – even anti-social types who are best avoided are employed and can afford chic holidays etc etc. I know that in other countries women stay at home but I have absolutely no idea what they do there.

Here, as soon as you're a couple of months old you go to nursery school – but I don't remember anything about that – and then you go to a kindergarten. I hated it. If there is any possibility of a group of people taking against me, they grab it with both hands. I used to think that this was because I'm ugly. But now I don't think that any more. Nearly everyone looks the same as me, with arms, legs, and all the other bits. I might be a little thin, but that can't be the straw that breaks the camel's back. So to speak. It's not because I'm particularly stupid and it's not because I'm the school nerd.

Now I'm beginning to think that whether you belong to a group or not is decided in the same way that animals decide. Those who belong to a group, who are always popular, who always have friends and who are always asked when a decision has to be made can sniff the sadness or loneliness of those who just DO NOT BELONG IN A GROUP. And no-one wants to have anything to do with them.

Although it's all perfectly sorted in my head now, it still isn't easy for me to stand around at every break and pretend that I'm very, very happy studying the various trees. Try acting relaxed and interested when you're not – the consequence is such extreme tension that you feel you will never move again or spit out a normal sentence. To finish off this train of thought I'd say: I've never missed my father, but I am lacking parents.

MAX   I look like something half-baked.

Everything about me is too long, and if a bit is mistakenly not too long, then it looks washed out. No-one would call me a looker. I'm standing in the kitchen, it's Sunday, fortunately my father has gone to the sports ground without me and I'm making myself spaghetti. I could eat spaghetti every day, and I usually do. Then I stare out of the window for a while just in case something really exciting happens. In front of the window is a desolate street and a thing that's pretending to be a park but is a million miles away from a really nice park. It's bloody cold, you can see that by the icy clouds that are just suspended behind the cars. It's so cold they're not even being blown away.

    I could do with a small car crash. I'd run down and free a thirteen-year old girl from the wreckage of the car. The parents would be dead, the girl confused. I'd keep her in my room and look after her until she's better. She'd probably be tied firmly into a wheelchair and I would push her through the pretend-park. She'd be so grateful that she'd fall in love with me. A beautiful girl with long hair and sad eyes due to the business with her parents and the wheelchair.

In my dreams. Instead nothing happens. I read for a bit and try to pretend that I live alone in the flat. I'd like that, but I'd be lying to myself: I know that my father will return home later on and it will become so unpleasantly silent that everything will seem to be covered with ice.

ANNA   Did I really never tell you about my mother?

My mother is not a shining example of an authority figure. I have a suspicion she doesn't know what on earth to do with a child. On the whole I find adults embarrassing, they question you intensively about things that they are not interested in at all: So, tell me, how's school? What do you enjoy playing? What's your favourite meal? They have absolutely no idea what interests young people and they don't have any idea how to talk to them. So, tell me, how was the office today? And how's the Party progressing? I mean, who on earth wants to know anything about that.

Ideally I'd like adults to talk about interesting things such as: do they think they might have been swapped as a child? Have they ever been to Amsterdam? Do they have the feeling they are being weighed down by the expectations of strangers? All the time I feel that everyone is expecting something of me but I have no idea what it is.

Now I'm losing the thread again.

My mother behaves in a way that could be described as tricky. She works in the Department of Culture — and there's really nothing else to be said about that. The riveting question is: for how much longer? My mother is developing a serious alcohol problem. Perhaps it doesn't belong in this journal but I don't want anything to be kept hidden. I sense that I am not alone in having a parent who drinks. It's probably so normal that no-one talks about it. Or else every-one is too ashamed. Like me.

Mother (in this country no-one would ever dream of calling their mother Claudia or Ingrid, even if it is their name. Parents are called mother and father and that's that). When mother comes home from work she's already a bit difficult. Often she sways about, as if on a ship, her eyes are wide open and she speaks absolutely correctly. I know straightaway that she's been drinking. She hates me then, I think, because she's ashamed. My mother drinks at work, at home, and with men she meets in bars. Until recently she took me with her on these little excursions.

I really want you to picture the scene. It was always a Sunday (and I believe you know what I think of Sundays) and by seven o'clock mother was hyper-excited and ready for the off. 'Come on, let's go for a walk,' was how it always started. Of course, I thought: cheers, bottoms up! As usual we'd set off down one of the three bridle paths there are around the town. It doesn't matter which one you follow all three lead to tedious castles with — abracadabra! — a bar next door. After we'd walked in silence and studied one of the three tedious castles, we'd head for the bar. First of all we'd eat something and drink some schnapps, and that would be the end of it. No power on earth could make my mother leave then. Soon a couple men would be sitting around the table and drinking while I just loitered next to them. At first I'd be bored but then I'd become miserable because I really did not like seeing my mother in that state.

Because by that point she just wasn't present any more. That's the awful thing: my mother departs from herself when she's drinking. That's what I hate the most, she becomes absent, she's no longer herself and no matter how hard I try I can never bring her back to where she's left me all on my own. Usually we'd sit in the bar until it was dark and then often one of the men would come home with us. (So, tell me, how is school going? What do you enjoy playing ...) They'd continue drinking in mother's room. I'd close the blinds, read and try not to hear the noise they'd be making.

And why did I not just get up and walk away from these excursions? It's obvious: I was afraid for my mother. I think that as a child you remain part of your mother for a long time even if you don't want to, and if one of you is doing something stupid then it always hurts the other. I'm not sure what could have happened to her. She might have been run over or she might have fallen down and died and left me all alone. I think these sorts of fears are shared by all children whose parents are divorced. There's nothing particularly significant about them. I don't have any specific phobias such as being held in a fearsome vice by a virus or being afraid that birds might pick the tiles off our roof and kidnap me ...

Close on the tail of being afraid that something might happen to mother comes being afraid of the shame. I hate it when other people laugh at my mother because she's swaying or talking too loudly. I don't want other people to see her like that.

We've given up on the walks. Mother now goes out on her own and every so often brings home drunken men who usually look ashamed when they see me. I've really no idea what's wrong with adults.

The saddest thing about my mother's drinking is that I just don't understand why she doesn't stop. It's not as if it's a lot of fun for her. She doesn't look better because of it and what's more she gets anxious and angry. The most awful thing is when she starts screaming at me the following morning. About everything. But actually it's because I'm there. And because she is there. If someone else was there then they'd feel the sharp edge of her tongue too. There's nothing worse than being shouted at first thing in the morning and not knowing why. It poisons the atmosphere, if I can put it that like that. I slink back into my room, but even then I'm not safe from her. Often she comes after me and goes on shouting.

I'm afraid of my mother when she's like that. That's when I just want her to be normal. I also want her to be normal when her speech is slurred and she looks glassy, or when she's making a noise with unsightly men. I've thrown away the alcohol, I've hidden it, I've fought with her and I've cried. But there's nothing I can do that makes any difference. Sometimes it's really shitty that as a child you simply can't get up and walk away.

MAX   Going outside is not a good idea either.

There's nothing about this town that appeals to me. I've definitely grown out of the playground phase, I mean, it's been ages since I found going down the slide and all that business exciting. Now a couple of times a year there's a big fair but it's always taken over by older kids who engage in moronic power games. They shove and they push each other – apparently hormones are responsible for turning teenage boys into cretins, at least that's what I read somewhere. Then of course there's the park, which is boring, and the Museum for Early History, which has models of Stone Age men squatting around a campfire. One thing's for sure, it didn't look much fun in the Stone Age. They must have been freezing.

So where was I?

Our flat is nice and warm. My policeman father gets coal for free, or something like that. I don't understand how anyone here can work for the police. He has to spy on people and arrest Rockers. Rockers are people who wear jeans, parkas, have long hair and don't want to fit in, which is fine by me. Who on earth wants to fit in with this moronic crap? When he does talk, my father enjoys giving me lectures on our wonderful country, a country that enables him, a child of simple peasants, to get the sort of fantastic job where he is allowed to maltreat sixteen-year-old enemies-of-the-State by putting them in handcuffs. Personally, I think our country's pretty unpleasant. In school they explain to us that we are locked in, well, of course they don't use the words LOCKED IN. The Wall, i.e. the Wall to protect us against the fascists, only exists because the people's enemy, i.e. the West, would attack us and sabotage everything otherwise. Excuse me, who actually believes that crap?

A country that locks up its inhabitants because it's afraid that if it doesn't they'll all run away needs its head examining.

I'm hoping that it will be Monday soon and I can go back to school. Not because I particularly like school but because every week that passes brings adulthood one step closer.

In the meantime it's dark outside, and quite visibly icy. I turn the radio on. Sad trumpet music. There's no decent music here apart from on Radio Luxembourg and the only records available are by groups from the GDR and Russia. About once a year there might be a record from a Western group and then hundreds queue overnight in front of the record shop to get hold of a record from Pink Floyd. I prefer to record Radio Luxembourg on cassette. The quality is pretty inferior but the music, proper music from Queen and David Bowie, can make you think you are somewhere else entirely.

I tell you what I want to be: grown up and living in a friendly country in an apartment full of books and decent music. Preferably with a beautiful wife in a wheelchair who tilts her head when she speaks to me.

Most of the time, I have to confess, I just feel lonely.

ANNA   Did I ever tell you about myself?

It seems to me that I've not existed for very long. I mean, as a person. When I see photo of myself when I was younger (I know that sounds ridiculous coming from a child) I can't work out what I was feeling at the time. I must have been like some vegetable. Meaning, I never thought about my appearance and I'm pretty sure a cucumber doesn't either. At least that is what I hope because it'd be completely stupid for a cucumber to want to look like a cauliflower, I mean, that's not the path to happiness is it?

In fact, I've only very recently started to be interested in my appearance. Or asked who I am, because I'm not so clear about that either. I look very ordinary. My hair colour is not, well, grey, but that sort of shade, in blonde. I'm tall and thin and there's nothing extraordinary about me. I'd really like to look like one of those girls from the children's books I used to love. They always had red hair, freckles and green eyes. They looked very striking and were brave souls. But personally I've not met a single girl who looked like that.

Each and every one of those girls in the books was an orphan. Glorious! I'm sure it makes everything much easier. All the children I know have to struggle with difficult parents. But when it comes to their adventures, I mean, please. I know that something has to happen in books but for heaven's sake, who on earth is always bumping into robbers on the street they absolutely have to unmask? Or magicians? Or conjuring thieves? I know not one.

I know that I wanted to tell you about myself but this time there is a good reason for rambling: there really is not much more to tell. Perhaps if I was elsewhere I could improve myself with more interesting clothes, but I live in the GDR and with the best will in the world I simply can't imagine more interesting clothes. The stuff in my size here is, without exception, foul. Revolting beige colours, or maybe something in blue, always some sort of pattern on the fabric, small boats or dice. I hate patterns. And I hate small boats.

By the way, I have to say that it's worse getting the wrong present than it is getting no presents at all. Recently my mother bought me a pair of trousers. She never buys me presents normally. A pair of pale blue cord trousers with boats all over them. I nearly cried. I felt so sorry for my mother that I wasn't delighted about them. It was terrible. I really hate disappointing people but I get the feeling there's no getting round it. There are some people who turn up somewhere all radiant, shiny and full of wit. I, on the other hand, turn up and it's as if I absorb the light and at the same time the air turns chilly. If I think of it like that, I must be disappointment made flesh to other people.

As I said, I have no idea who I am or what others think of me. I think that most people view me the way they view a chair. A not particularly exquisite chair at that. Just a wooden chair hanging around. At least if we're talking about me in closed rooms. If I was a chair out on the street I'd cause too much chaos. Outside I'm much more like a park bench with snow gently falling on it. A little grandma with a red hooded cape would sit on me and what the little grand-ma would like to do above all else in the world is feed the birds that are loitering around her. Instead they all fly away and the little grandma would be left alone again. Or something like that.

I am already taller than my mother. And nearly everyone else in my class. But half as fat as everyone else I know. Sadly this is not down to any particularly exciting health issue. I'd have no problem at all living in a sanatorium – in France. There'd be white beds on bright verandas that have a few small windows. I'd lie in bed with my serious illness and read, and worried nurses would ask me about my condition. In French of course. But I'd be too weak to reply …

I have a thing about beds. The most wonderful thing in the world would be to travel abroad in my bed. We would tour around together at a stately speed. But where would we go? And so we're back where we started.

MAX   I did go away once.

On holiday with my father. We went to the Harz mountains. Well, they're so-called low mountains. Low mountains are the ones too cowardly to grow but equally they're too cowardly to be a plain. The great average. Whatever.

We stayed in a holiday home. There are hardly any hotels or cars or planes in the GDR. You go on holiday by train and you go to a holiday home run by your employer. You stay in a room with a washbasin that has a slight resemblance to a hospital ward and three times a day you go down to the dining room to eat. But of course there's no buffet — everyone gets the same food served straight onto the plate. During the day you go rambling. As you know, there's nothing children like better than to go rambling with their parents followed by skittles in the evening. Or listening to some singing group. Or watching some amateur theatre. We've all been there and done that.

Before we set off I always think that holidays are a great idea. That lasts about two days. My father is the same as he is at home but it's harder work because we have to hang out together twenty-four hours a day. I would love it if he would talk to me as if to a friend or a son even, or at the very least to a friendly dog. Once when we were out on a walk I thought for about an hour or so about simply grabbing hold of his hand. Then I actually did it. It felt completely wrong and my father pulled his hand away really fast, as if he'd accidentally touched something revolting.

I could have died with embarrassment. On one holiday, I think I must have been about ten, I kept on seeing a girl in the dining room and then at the boring evening events. A lovely girl. I kept on thinking about her and looking out for her. That was really the highlight of the holiday and the first time I'd ever been interested in a girl. But I don't think she'd even noticed I existed.

Sometimes, and here I really am admitting to a weakness, I would like to have a friend. Someone I could talk to. Or even better, someone I'd get on so well without having to talk to them. At the time I thought it was bound to have been like that with the girl. We would guess each other's thoughts while I was holding her hand. I mean, permanent thought-guessing while holding hands is roughly the most exciting thing I can imagine. Of course I'll never see the girl again.

ANNA   Did I ever tell you that I'd never dream of making up friends?

No way would I think of giving my diary a name. Hello, dearest Elfi, it's lovely to be able to write to you again. Yuck. It's already embarrassing enough that I'm talking to myself in writing.

I would have liked to have a girlfriend, but none ever turned up.

A girl did show interest in me once. She was unbelievably short and trembled all the time. If she'd been a dog she'd have been a whippet. The girl really wanted to spend time with me and I'd have liked nothing better than to have liked her. So we did the sort of things that friends do. We had the odd sleepover, mucked about, things like that. From my point of view it was a disaster. I didn't know what to say to the girl so I talked rubbish at her non-stop to cover up the silence. I told her stories about cranes and construction vehicles that come to life at night and build buildings that terrify people. There's some competition — who can build the worst building. And that's how the Palast der Republik in Berlin and other spectacular buildings came to be built.

Then the quaking girl would say, 'Is that really true?' or 'What do you mean?' Killed everything stone dead.

You never feel quite so alone as you do when you're with someone you think is that special friend, but neither of you understands the other. The girl lived in the Abraham-Lincoln-Strasse, I'll never forget that. I imagined Lincoln to be just like her, dried up and considered. I felt so pressurised because she didn't mean anything to me. So then I finished with her. And that gave me no satisfaction either. I never again want to be in the embarrassing situation of having to finish with someone. But that's something else.

The only others in my intimate circle of friends — apart from the girl — were two dogs. One of them was a stuffed dog, so completely squashed and battered that it looked like a sheep. I used to tie a lead around it and pull it behind me, bobbing along. I talked to it and felt real emotion towards it. This went on till about two years ago. Embarrassing or what? So let's talk about something else.

After the stuffed dog I had a real live dog that I got from the animal protection league. The dog was brought up on a farm and was scared witless. But you know what girls are like, they think that a bit of kindness sorts everything out. The dog's name was Robbi and on the farm he'd been tied him up in such a way that he'd had to sleep standing up. Plus other forms of cruelty. So there you have it, he was raving bonkers and had no idea about people while I, on the other hand, had no idea about dogs. One thing led to another. I pictured myself running across fields in a gentle breeze with my friend, the dog. But the long and the short of it … it was just like the girl from the Lincoln Strasse: I didn't understand the dog and he didn't understand me. He didn't want me to cuddle him and was always pooing in the flat. So we separated.

MAX   Monday at last.

I have to go to school and I hate it. I hate the teachers, I hate the light in the classrooms, I hate the boredom, the sound the chalk makes on the blackboard and the breaks, during which it is obvious to the blind that no-one wants to talk to me, or – to make myself sound more interesting – that I wish to be left alone. I hate the sandwich I've brought with me and I hate the milk we have to drink because it's good for you. You make a hole in the aluminium top and then drink, but the milk tops smell of old milk. I hate the Pioneer assemblies because they're just rubbish. When you start school you're given a white shirt, a blue necktie and a revolting cap. Pioneers are like little soldiers, or whatever, I've never quite understood. It's all about turning young people into responsible citizens with the right political attitude. Every Monday we have Flag Assembly. This is when you have to wear the Pioneer crap, salute the flag and sing songs. What sort of nonsense is that? I hate sport because all boys pretend to be tough, barge into each other and must never ever show any pain. I hate mornings, because the whole day lies ahead of me. I hate learning Russian because you're never going to speak Russian to anyone, travelling to Russia is expensive and the only Russians here are soldiers who refuse to speak to us, and I wouldn't know what to say anyway. I hate the dog I have to walk past on the way to school that always, and I mean always, barks and one day is bound to jump over the fence. I hate the older kids who stand around in groups, smoke and pretend to be important. I hate the fact I have to walk past them to get into school and then I'm shit scared and hate myself for it. I hate it when the bell for break rings and always makes me jump. I hate it when the teacher pulls me out of my reverie with some saying or another that only a teacher would think is witty. I hate the fact I'm tired when school is over and I have to go home, where it's cold until I light the fire and make something to eat. But apart from that, everything else is hunky-dory.

ANNA   Did I ever tell you about school?

Today is Monday. Don't ask how I survived Sunday. Actually, ask away. If only someone would ask me something. I did some writing and looked out of the window. Where on earth can a child without friends go on a cold Sunday? Wander through the streets? Look at foodstuffs in the shop windows? Sounds super. My mother never cooks. During the week I eat at school, at home I make myself tomato puree sandwiches, which are better than they might sound. I'm not particularly interested in food. I just eat whatever.

Above all else, going to school means: how can I make myself invisible? I love rain because then I can hide under an umbrella. Winter's okay too, because everyone's wearing thick horrible clothes and it's dark in the morning (on the way to school) and in the evening (on the way back). Apart from the fact that I feel as ugly as sin, I've also got the relevant gear, cord trousers that are too short and a scratchy, woolly jumper. In green. Green is number two after yellow in the revolting-colour Olympics.

A couple of girls in my class have CONTACTS IN THE WEST, which means that they have relatives in West Germany who send them things that make everyone else madly jealous. Most children assume automatically that you're a better person if you own a pair of jeans. You can't get jeans here but we all know that they're the hippest thing to wear. I can only fantasise about owning a pair of jeans. It's worse in the summer because as a girl you have to wear a skirt and I look absolutely terrible – my legs are too thin and then there's the sock business ... in fact, please don't go there.

Everyone is in love with one particular girl in my class. Of course she has a pair of jeans, she also has breasts and hair that she blow-dries with a flick. Her face is very sweet and she's going out with a boy three classes above us. During break she stands in the play-ground with him and they kiss. Is that right? No boy would dream of kissing me. In my class they're all at least six inches shorter than I am. But me getting an older boy is on a par with me getting a pair of jeans: NO CHANCE.

I am interested in boys. On the whole. Not that I've the least idea what you do with them. But you can be interested in them nonetheless. Sadly I'm not very quick-witted, nor am I funny, nor am

I pretty. In short, there's nothing much about me that might interest a boy.

I presume it's nice to have boyfriend. I wouldn't want to hang around the playground kissing him though, I'd much rather run away. Wearing a large hat. Foreign countries, adventures, all far, far away. Whatever. This boy and girl thing is a real puzzle. I'm not sure what they do when they go out. Usually they shove each other a bit and stand around in silence. Which is not the answer either. I can do silence perfectly well on my own.

In case I haven't mentioned it, I'm not Miss Popular in my school. But apart from community activities I don't have to work too hard to get by. My grades are okay. It's a much more difficult thing to get through a whole school day without falling asleep. Particularly at lunchtime, when all I want to do is fall over and sleep under the table. Often I get the feeling that my entire body is made up of boredom molecules. It's exhausting trying to concentrate when nearly every subject bores me. Sometimes I'm brave enough to read a book under the desk, but that's not the solution either.

I don't understand what purpose geometry or the periodic table will serve later on in life. Will they be vital to life? Maybe perhaps when you meet an alien. They might say 'sdlhfdsjkkhlyrhcnsp'; which means, 'Tell us how you calculate a scalene triangle and we will refrain from experimenting on your spleen.'

What I loathe most is sports. It might sound banal but the whole bloody business of the two sportiest kids choosing their teams happens every single time. And it's always the same kids who are left over, like old gym shoes: the fat, the short and the peculiar. The same humiliation every single sports lesson. I dream of the day when I'm an adult and able to really take my revenge. How I've no idea. I'll think of something when the time comes. One thing I know for sure, it will have nothing to do with irregular triangles.

People say that school is preparation for life. That is perfectly true: all the unjust things that adults do to each other, well, children do exactly the same. There are the show-offs, the aggressors, the clowns, the donkeys and the fat girls who like a good fight. Some children will always be hit. Every day. For no reason apart from the fact that people are vile. They always torment the weak whenever the opportunity arises.

Whatever might happen to me I will never torment anyone else. That's what I've resolved. I think there's no point in being nasty to other people. I think you turn evil when you lie, betray people and put them under pressure. I want to be an unobtrusive, quiet person who never disturbs anyone else or takes their chair away. That's sort of what I think.

MAX   Summer never happened.

In the middle of winter it's just as difficult to imagine that it might warm up at some point as it is to remember how revolting it is to have a cold when you're feeling just fine. When I walk to school in the morning the streets are full of tired adults. They all look as if they would like to cry. Just the crunching of their footsteps in the snow and the daylight that's not really there. Some mornings I'm afraid that I will grow up and that everything will be just the same as it is now. No miracle in sight. I just can't picture much joy or any surprises. A holiday in a holiday home certainly isn't one. Perhaps that's why everyone marries so young, because they dream that their own fresh lives will improve things. And then they sit around in their own fresh apartments attempting to be adult and understand how everything works, but they have no idea. Instead they get old thinking about it, the walls turn yellow and everything is as before.

ANNA   Did I ever tell you that school's not exactly exciting either?

After school I go home, make myself a pile of sandwiches, lie on my bed and eat them in the company of cultivated reading matter. Outside nothing's changed. Grey. Just as I pick up the eighth slice, there is a ring at the door. A boy I've never seen before is standing there. Which doesn't mean anything, because what with my old war wound, I can't see much at all any more. Okay, that's a lie. Standing on the doorstep is a boy who looks like a girl. Well he looks more like a girl than I do.

MAX   Walking home is not much fun.

After school I walk past the stupid dog, which of course starts barking, and think up various delicious doggy recipes. Baked dog with sage, dog on a spit with an onion in its mouth … I arrive home just as I'm experimenting with dog in a pastry jacket and see a woman collapse in a heap on the pavement. I try to help her but she is babbling oddly and is not at all interested in standing up. The situation is beyond me. In my social circle I don't generally have to deal with women who've collapsed.

I'm fairly sure she's the mother of the girl who lives one floor below us and who occasionally looks out of the window. I've never thought about her very much. She doesn't seem particularly inviting. Not the sort of person who immediately begins to tell you the story of their life. But I'm guessing it's her mother and I can't simply leave her lying on the street. I'd like to see that, someone whistling as they step over a mother lying on the ground. There's not another soul about, so I go up to the girl's apartment hoping that she's home and that she has some idea about what to do with her mother.

ANNA   Did I ever tell you that my mother falls over now and then?

My mother is actually lying in the street. Not run over or anything like that, just a bit dazed. At least that's what I say to the boy who lives in our block and whom I've never seen before. The truth of course is that mother is drunk. We drag her into the apartment and that's so exhausting that I don't have the energy to be embarrassed.

After we've laid her on her bed, I sit with the boy in my cold room. I've no idea why he's sitting here and not slipping back to his super parents in his super warm apartment where there's probably a hot meal waiting on the table. My last sandwich is sitting on my bed. As if he could read my mind the boy says, 'I don't really want to go up to our flat, there's no-one there anyway. Can I stay a bit longer?' I mean, what can I say to that: No, buzz off. However you can pick up my mother any time you find her lying around?

But I don't think the boy was expecting a reply. He looked at my books, most of which he knew. He'd also read Edgar Allan Poe and we agree that he's definitely not suitable reading material for children. For months after reading the book we were both afraid of being buried alive. And had nightmares about waking up in a coffin and not being able to get out and no-one hearing us. I used to leave a piece of paper next to my bed saying that if I died in the middle of the night I wanted to be cremated.

As if my mother would have taken any notice of such an appeal.

The boy watches the white clouds that come out of his mouth when he breathes out and I look at my feet because I find the whole thing quite difficult, and maybe also because I have no idea what to say to a boy. He asks me if I want to go up to his flat and eat spaghetti because my mother probably needs a good rest. She certainly does, I think to myself, we can hear her snoring next door. I like the fact that the boy expresses himself so thoughtfully and as a result I don't really feel embarrassed by the noise my mother is making.

So I go up one floor with the boy, who's called Maximilian, to a neat and tidy apartment that has a curious silent quality. A different sort of silent to our flat. Ours is unconscious, his apartment seems more like it's frozen.

First we eat some spaghetti that the boy cooks very professionally, and then we go into his room, which looks like my room only in warm.

Perhaps both rooms belong to nutcases, I think, while having a look around at what's there. The room looks like a girl's room in a man's flat. No, even worse, like a girl's room in a barracks. Not that there are dolls flying around or pink stuff everywhere, but everything is cosy and nicely furnished. I feel at home in this sort of room.

We sit on the boy's sofa, the sort of foldaway sofa that turns into a bed at night. The sales hit of the GDR. In every, and I mean every, single apartment you will find one of those stupid sofas in blue or red. There are no other colours.

And suddenly we start to talk. It's so strangely simple that I only really notice that it's got dark and three hours have flown by when Maximilian goes to make cocoa. I consider going back to mother but I never want to leave this boy's room. I feel just the way I feel when I'm on my own. I'm not watching myself from the outside. Which is strange.

MAX   It's very strange.

I might well have completely overlooked Anna if her mother had not chosen to collapse on that particular day, the day I left school a few seconds later than usual because I was thinking up recipes for dog. The dog gave me a friend. So I'm not going to cook him, instead I'm going to let him loose in a wood to be with his brothers, the wolves, and his friends, the grizzly bears. He'll have a fair chance of surviving then.

If you meet a grizzly bear, it's best to pretend to be dead. This was one of the subjects I discussed with Anna. Every night she checks under her bed in case there are people there. But apart from that she's completely normal, she knows that aliens experiment on the citizens of the GDR and she also has a couple of recipes for dog. At some point she went back to her apartment and to her mother. I don't know what's worse, a father who says nothing or a mother who's in the habit of – let's say – falling over. We didn't make a date for any particular time. I'm bound to see her again because I know where she lives.

I was washing up the cocoa mugs when I realised that I hadn't cooked anything and that my father would be home any minute. And all at once I'd had it up to here, I can't tell you how it felt. Standing alone in that kitchen and knowing I had to live another six years with my father, a man who wouldn't even hold my hand. I became so unbelievably weary thinking of all those years that lay ahead that I felt like collapsing on the spot. And I know what happens to people who collapse. They get dragged into apartments by children.

So I pack a few things in a bag and walk down a floor. I leave the lights on.

ANNA   Did I ever tell you how awful it can be, being a child?

Back in our apartment I feel even more stupid than usual. Maybe it's because the last few hours were really lovely. Or perhaps because I wasn't all on my own, for a change.

Snoring sounds come from my mother's bedroom. This is starting to happen more frequently, she does something stupid and then she falls asleep while I sit there and get cross, or feel alone, and I'm cold. There is no-one I can turn to in these situations.

My father has a new family. I went there once. My father's new son played some sort of instrument, I can't remember what, probably he plays lots of different instruments as he's so very gifted. Father's new wife was perfectly-groomed and everything smelt good. I just didn't fit in it at all, with my awful clothes, my too-long arms and my ash-coloured hair. And they were all so over-nice to me, completely fake, saying things like: Would you like some tea and biscuits? And tell us, how school is going? My mother was so totally not talked about, that it stood out like a sore thumb. When I left, I felt like a small dirty dog that had made a puddle indoors. Actually I've no idea how a dog feels, it just came out like that. In case a dog should read my notes in the future: don't be cross!

So, what was I saying? My mother's sleeping and suddenly I feel completely knackered. I sit on the window seat in my room, which is where I always sit when I feel knackered, and I know what's going to happen next. At some stage my mother will wake up and come into my room full of remorse. She'll be so embarrassed she won't look me square in the eye but over my shoulder. It's the look of someone who knows they've made a right mess of things. Then later on I'll go to bed and know even now what that feels like, the first fifteen minutes in a cold and slightly damp bed, and then at some stage I'll fall asleep, get up early next morning, in the cold, and head off to school. I've really had it up to here.

Then the doorbell rings. Well who knows, maybe my father's just fallen over. That would liven things up.

MAX   I talk about my life.

I tell Anna that we have to get away. Right now this second. Because it's winter and because everything's a pain. And she has to come with me because she's not happy either, and no-one but no-one can wait another six years in this hell-hole to come of age. I tell her that she needs to bring her identity papers with her (that's the policeman's son in me); and that we'll think of some reason why we have to go to Bulgaria, to visit an uncle or something, and then we'll hitchhike down south and then flee by boat to Italy or Greece or just somewhere that's not like here. But I don't have to say all that. After a couple of sentences Anna says: okay. She packs a few things, fetches some money from who knows where and then we leave. She leaves the lights on.

ANNA   Did I ever tell you how I ran away?

Running away suits me just fine. I'm not really a brave person, but in some situations you just have to forget you're a coward and get on with it. Another three months of winter, another however many years of mother collapsing and then being alone at school — those are just not good alternatives. So I don't give them a second thought. There's nothing to lose. If I decide after a day or two that I'd rather be a coward then I can always come back. (Ha, at least that's what I'm thinking now, but perhaps the door to my room will be bricked up, which is what they do in the West to people who are given the sack. At least that's what we're told here.) And I think I can be certain that that my mother would have woken up by then.

I pack very sensible things. A warm pullover, a sleeping bag and a mini tent. All the sorts of things that I know from reading are essential for running away. I don't leave a note for mother. Nothing. I don't even care where we go to and what we'll do there. I just want to get away.

As if I am no longer present, I am steered by aliens out of the apartment, down the stairs and onto the street. It's the first time ever that I don't think but just do. What a great feeling, not being weighed down by fear and thinking you have to do something. I recommend it. I read once that this is how men get through most of their lives. It must be fantastically simple being a man.

We run with our backpacks through the dark town. If anyone were to film us now, it would be a film about refugee children. Probably one from Russia.

The buildings around us are all grey and cold. Behind the windows people sit on identical furniture because they have no choice, and read or drink something or listen to the radio. The buildings are all grey, by the way, because the paint's come off and there's no new paint available to buy. And should some ever become available then no-one buys it because the buildings all belong to the state. If things don't belong to people then they don't feel responsible for them. But I think I've said that already.

It's certainly no joke running away from this country. People who run away live dangerously. Every now and then one of them is shot but usually they end up in prison. Of course officially no-one will say what happened to them. We simply learnt that fugitives from the German

Democratic Republic are enemies of the state. I am afraid. Not of becoming an enemy of the state, that's just rubbish, but of the police and the army. A long time ago when I was in Berlin with my mother we went to look at the Wall. After a couple of seconds, two solders came along and yelled at us: come on, on your way now, chop chop! Just at that moment I looked over to the West. People were standing on one of the watch-towers waving to us. They were just a few metres away. The space in-between however was chock-a-block with mines, concrete, barbed wire and dogs. To protect us. What else.

We head off through the night towards the motorway. It's so bizarrely simple between us. Maximilian tells me about Italy, about how warm it is there and how we will be adopted by one of the Doge's successors. He talks about his room, which he will be able to decorate exactly how he likes. It will have a huge door through to the veranda and on the veranda there will be a horse. Not that he's interested in riding on into old age but for reasons of taste there will simply have to be a white horse on the veranda.

It's not quite seven but the town is al-ready dead as a dodo. Perhaps my mother's waking up now and has no idea of who she is or where I am. It's going to take a while before the police start hunting for us. I think it's great that

I am thinking in such a professional manner. It's like I run away from home every day. I ask myself, what I will remember in the future when I am who knows where in some warm country. The white clouds forming in front of my mouth? The smouldering rubbish?

I've no idea what two children can do in Italy but we'll have to wait and see. Perhaps you grow up faster in dangerous situations. At last we reach the spur road onto the motorway. But regrettably no car has driven past in the last half an hour.

nameless street

MAX   No cars here.

But at least there is a streetlight. So we stand underneath it, in the hope it will warm us up. Which it fails to do. Better and better. I put on my father face, tilt my head slightly to one side and look up and down. Then I examine the map of Eastern Europe and nod my head. I see.

No idea what to do next. Plan A is done and dusted. There is no plan B. It's odd. If I was on my own now I'd turn around and go back home and somehow convince myself I'd taken a remedial walk. But there's a girl standing next to me and somehow I just can't be the first one to give up. So I say: all we have to do is travel in a south-easterly direction. Poland, Hungary, Romania, Bulgaria. It doesn't look that far and you can certainly do four countries in a week. Well you can if a car comes along. Which is not looking likely at present.

It's too cold to snow. The ground is frozen so that it crackles. We jump up and down on the spot and keep stumm because our faces are so cold and it just sounds weird talking. Like an automaton. Far away a dog barks (yum yum: dog stew). Over there are a couple of small houses that must mark the first village away from the town. It smells of cows. There's a huge dairy-herd facility nearby. That's what they're called here. There's no such thing as a small farm with a few animals, instead everything is gathered together in large conglomerates. The animals are housed in huge buildings and the farmers don't look like farmers at all, they don't have dirndls or that sort of thing, instead they wear worn-out old clothes and headscarves. Even the men. No, that's nonsense, men wear those stupid hats of course. But at the moment there's not a living soul in sight. Everything is completely dead.

Finally a car comes along, a Trabant. We first hear it when it's miles away. Then we listen to it get closer, watch it drive past us and sail gaily off into the darkness. Yup, he'll soon regret missing out on the company of two such fasci-nating people. Then I begin a conversation with my feet simply to keep the blood flowing. You know it's all over when you fall asleep in the cold. Don't fall sleep feet. Did I ever tell you ...

ANNA Did I ever tell you how strong-willed am?

My patience came as a complete surprise. I'm beginning to think I'm a very relaxed, almost brave person. I quickly build a monument to myself in the centre of the town. Life-sized, with a sabre in my hand, on a horse.

I don't know how long we've been standing here but I'm beginning to lose all sensation. But do we have a choice? Return home, where it's no warmer and my mother's snoring away? The lack of any warm spot could well make me unhappy, so I rein in my thoughts.

One hundred hours later and after at least ten cars have driven past the mad fools we are, a lorry stops. We only realise that he has stopped because of us when he beeps his horn. We had completely given up on the idea that something might actually happen tonight. As we run towards the lorry I suddenly feel a stab of fear. Hideous overwhelming terror. It's actually happening, we're on our way. Is this what I really want? I start to shake. So embarrassing.

Even my teeth are chattering, but that might be because of the cold.

The man sitting in the cabin of the lorry seems much too small for such a large vehicle. Like a child in the wrong clothes. He has bad teeth but very nice eyes and has to go as far as the Polish border. At least that's what I think he says because I think he is speaking Polish. He says something like Graniza. Ok, Graniza it is.

We crawl in behind the driver onto a sort of bed. He mutters something like, aha, grab a cover and tuck yourselves in, and then the lorry huffs. Either that or we've just driven over a very large air-filled animal. We're off. The animal is left lying sprawled across the road.

Travelling is so meditative. At least that's what I say to my many friends. You are moved about in peace. And quiet. If only all of life was like that. The driver is very pleasant, he asks no questions and doesn't talk, the radio is playing Polish music and the motorway is empty. Probably another atom bomb. I'm too tired to speak.

The driver gives us a thermos flask with peppermint tea in and a couple of sandwiches. Very good bread, very healthy, with cheese. It is so warm in the driver's cabin and snug under the cover that I doze off. I don't fall into a proper deep sleep, but nod off into a heavy doze.

I think about Bulgaria where it's bound to be warm and where there's a sea. Not a sad grey puddle like the Baltic Sea (another thing that's grey). Did I ever tell you about the time I went on holiday with my mother to the Baltic Sea? It was last year and the last time I went away with her. I was so happy before we set off. The really peculiar thing is that children up to a certain age are always happy when they can be together with their parents. As if we are nothing more than an extension of their bodies. Or is it just me who is over-clingy?

We didn't have to stay in a holiday home but were put up in a private house. For the East it was fairly romantic, a house with garden and a veranda. I was very happy for the first couple of days. I ran around by the sea with my mother and it was warm and smelled heavenly. I had never been to the seaside before. There were pine trees or maybe fir trees – the ones with needles that are only found there – and it smelled lovely when you were near them. In the evening we went back to the holiday home to eat and after that we sat in the dark in swinging wicker chairs.

On the third evening we went to a restaurant to eat. Schnapps arrived on the table, followed by a man who I guessed was the local village assi. (Assi stands for Asocial. They're the ones who don't work – in a country where everyone works. This is just to assist future generations.) The guy looked like a zombie with yellow teeth, a moustache and a squint. My mother began to drink schnapps with him and to giggle. I was beside myself with embarrassment. They were still sitting there when the place closed. My mother staggered out onto the street and the guy stumbled along beside us. I could have screamed at him. I could have killed him. Well, probably not. Where on earth is a child going to put a corpse by the Baltic Sea?

And from that evening on that's how the holiday went. Mother saw the cretin every day, she purchased vodka from the shop, was glassy and not quite there. I spent most of my time sitting alone on the beach, reading a bit and trying to persuade myself that I was very happy in the sunshine by the sea. And it worked, sort of.

MAX   The night speeds past.

I don't sleep because Anna is sleeping and one of us has to stay on our toes. However harmless the lorry driver appears to be it's quite possible that he's a child smuggler or something like that, you hear such unsavoury things about hitchhiking. I'm a little afraid. Now I can admit it. Well, maybe it's not exactly fear. But one thing is certain, I am not relaxed.

At some point soon the lorry will stop, we will get out and have to sort out our future. Adults know automatically what to do. I've no idea how. There are so many things that need to be done in order to live: rent a flat, get a passport, a career and insurance. Mustn't let myself go there. I am now an adventurer. Samoa and all that.

It's warm and pleasant right now. The man doesn't smoke, instead he quietly hums Polish songs and now and then checks whether we're asleep or not. When he sees that I'm awake, he offers me tea, bread and sweets. There's no doubt he has children himself, he knows exactly what to do: don't irritate and always offer food.

I force myself to think about my father. I should try to develop a bad conscience. I imagine him sitting all alone at the table with probably only sandwiches to eat because he can't cook. After that he'll put on his policeman's hat, pick up his pistol and walk out of the house. I've no idea whether he'll miss me or not. What I mean is, will he feel anything apart from a sense that his routine's out of sync? I don't miss him, and that makes me feel sad. Right at this moment, on the road to nowhere.

ANNA   Did I ever tell you how horrible it is to wake up in a lorry?

Waking up is really unpleasant. I'm completely stiff and groggy as I tumble out of the lorry and stand around in the grey cold morning. Somewhere. I've no idea where. All I can see is an empty road, a sort of barracks and a grey sky. And for one minute I feel completely desperate. Is this really what the rest of my life is going to be like? Sleeping in lorries and being smelly and hungry and tired and ice-cold?

Come along child, I say to myself, it could be much worse. In Africa they don't even have money.

And we have a couple of hundred marks that I'd been saving because I wasn't sure how much longer my mother would keep her job. But at this very moment the money is not going to help because there's nothing here to spend it on. That's a lie, there is a service station in the barracks but it doesn't open for another hour.

'We're nearly at the border,' says Maximilian, and it sounds as if he's trying to be brave. It doesn't exactly draw me in. A border.

I'm not so naïve that I think a line drawn across the landscape by people means that on the other side there will suddenly be fruit trees in blossom and clear springs where young lambs gambol and drink.

Are children even allowed to cross borders? The fact is that children are not really allowed to do anything. It's as if they are not people but house pets. Dependent on adults. Which is totally absurd when you look at the adults we have to deal with.

I could try to make myself older. I could pretend to be an adult in order to gain respect, rent a flat, get a job as a cashier and so on and so forth. But sadly I don't have the foggiest idea how to do that. Probably something with wigs. But who on earth has access to a wig at a service station early in the morning?

Max and I are sitting fairly silently in front of the service station. There's no-one about. There's a couple of lorries in the car park, I imagine their drivers sleeping inside their cabins, toasty warm. I think it's about 300 degrees below zero. After we've been sitting there for a couple of years, the worst is over. My body perks up and I begin to think: it's not all bad. Soon the service station will open, we'll drink something hot and then carry on in a car and at some stage we will arrive where it's warm. Not to worry. I think that you can get used to many things and right now I'm coming to terms with living on the road.

Just as I was about to have a vision of Joan of Arc or Red Zora or whoever our Polish driver comes back round the corner. He gets very excited in Polish, apparently we're being stupid children, and he shoos us back into his lorry. He just went to the toilet. So here we are again in his lorry. Tea, but no more sandwiches. After a while he signals that we should follow him, the service station is open. I have to say that the first part of our journey has not gone at all badly.

MAX   Our first breakfast in freedom.

The service station is unbelievably warm. Tough-looking drivers get down from their lorry beds looking bedraggled. Most of them are Poles, a couple come from countries whose language I can't catch. They are all our new friends. Even though the service station has been open just six minutes they've successfully managed to fill it with smoke. I feel like Hansel and Gretel. Well one of them anyway. All we need now is red knitted caps and to hold tight onto each other's mittens.

A fat lady gives us tea and scrambled eggs and our mood improves no end. She talks to one of the men. Then she tells us that a man who is due to drive through a fair section of Poland will take us with him. Well that's that sorted. The man gives a wave, he is incredibly fat and looks okay.

We eat and eat and I notice that my stomach is getting bigger and bigger. I'm about to burst. What a way to go: burst at the seams while in a service station just short of Poland. Then everything happens very quickly. The man gets up, beckons to us, we say goodbye to our nice driver and the nice fat woman. We don't have to pay a thing. I've been told that the Germans are not particularly nice to their children, and right now I almost believe it's true: I get the feeling from these foreigners that they really treasure children.

Our new driver looks, and there's no other way of putting it, like a huge orang-utan. He's hairy all over, and sweaty, and everything about him gobbles and wobbles and wibbles. There's no nice bed in his lorry, just a bench and outside it's getting light. We travel with the man to the border. The policeman casts a glance into the cabin. I think he must be tired, or freezing, in any case we're of no interest to him at all. The houses running down the sides of the Polish streets look even more pitiful than the houses back home.

At some stage while we're driving along in silence I study Anna from the side. She is really cool for a girl. Doesn't pester you and talk rubbish. Did I ever tell you that I'm very sensitive to people talking rubbish? Anna might be a strange person but I have the feeling that one day we'll get on really well. Besides, I'm aware when I look at her that she's really beautiful from the side. Her nose is lovely and her hair falls at an angle over her eyes. She's the sort of girl that gets more beautiful the more you get to know her. There are the sort of 'five-minute' girls, the ones you just fall for and get over quickly. And then there are the evergreen girls, the ones you overlook at the beginning. Those are the ones you have to get used to until you become aware of their beauty. Well, I think I put that pretty well for a boy my age, one who's never had a girl.

I could be having the most unbelievable thoughts but for the fat man who's talking non-stop. Talking complete gibberish. His German is good and he's starting to get on my nerves a bit. No, he's getting on my nerves a lot. Every time my thoughts start to turn into a film that I'd like to see, he interrupts with some comment. We learn, without even wanting to, that he has a wife and two children, that he lives near the border with Hungary and that he misses his family when he's away. He asks us if our parents know where we are, and we both reply at the same time. In the sort of way that a master of interrogation would know immediately that we're lying, and lying badly. We must practice. But the fat man doesn't ask any more. Maybe he doesn't understand enough German for such delicate nuances. Even so, he asks a lot of questions about our relatives, what town we come from and so on. What's he keep asking for? Maybe he's really bored or something.

The road is also excruciatingly boring. Run down grey houses, unhappy trees. Every so often we stop at a service station and get a fizzy drink and at lunchtime, soup. It snows without stopping, small sharp flakes that don't stay. The sky hangs low and it's getting semi-dark again, although it has not been bright all day. There's something unreal about this drive. You don't have to make any decisions, you're not cold, you can't move and you get dangerously tired. Why did I think 'dangerously' just now?

And bang, I'm snatched out of my thoughts by the driver's voice again. The man is saying that he'll be home in half an hour. That it's a fair way to the border, particularly now in the dark, so it might be better to spend the night with him. Is that okay? That's what the man says and I think: oh shit. Going to the house of a strange man is really not the sort of thing you should do as a child. Even if you are two children.

It's quite clear that the man is a fair bit stronger than we are. Perhaps once we're in his house he'll put us out, with drops or something, and then do experiments on us. Or tie us up. And after that do experiments on us. Anna and I don't say a word but we look at each other and I notice that she's as uneasy as I am, but at the same time she's fairly keen on a bed. When the fat man mentions his two children again and that they'd be happy to see us, I look into Anna's eyes and see that we should accept the offer. So we leave the main road and set off into the darkness. Was this really such a good idea?

ANNA   Did I ever say that it's a bit odd going home a strange man?

I don't really like staying over with people I don't know. Although I have to say honestly that I've never been asked to stay over with people I don't know. Nor with people I do know for that matter.

The fat man looks sad in a comic sort of way. I can't describe it any better than that as I only know my way of being sad. He gives the impression of a person who has no feeling of connection to anything he does.

Now we're driving through a wood. At least, I think it's a wood, the light is fading and I can only see trees caught in the headlights. Behind them is some dark mass. Mustn't think about what that might be. I go quite stiff. I look at Max. He looks so funny and rigid. I don't think either of us has the nerve to say: 'Stop right now!' and then leap out of the cab and into the woods. I mean, you've got to decide to do that sort of thing. There's probably nothing creepy at all. It's simply dark outside, which happens, you know.

After quarter of an hour we spot some lights coming from a house. The fat man stops. You can only just see the outline of the house. The door opens and in the doorway stands a very, very thin woman, who waves at the fat man and us. We climb down, and the odd feeling lessens a bit. At least there's a woman here. She speaks German too and immediately I don't like her. She looks very dried out, like a sort of vegetable. Well, vegetables you find in East German greengrocers.

We go into the house, at least it's warm inside. The woman talks in Polish to the fat man. He laughs, so does she, then she pushes us into the kitchen and like a mad woman begins to fetch things out of the cupboards and put them on the table. Salami and stuff. I mean, please, who eats salami nowadays? Everyone knows it's unhealthy. The table groans with the weight of everything on it: soup and potatoes and vegetables and pirogi.*

We sit down and start to eat. What else should we do? Maybe it's poisoned, I think, but I just can't stop eating. How can anyone cook so well and be so thin? The woman is nothing but bones. She sits down next to us, which is not particularly appetising. It's like eating while being watched by a large bird. And she begins to ask us questions. She wants to know everything: how old we are, who are our parents, school, friends, where we're off to, who's waiting for us there. It's not a cosy chat between strangers, it's like being interrogated by the Inquisition.

We stutter and mumble, get caught up in bad excuses if not actual lies, and I can see she's not fooled by it all. She cracks the bones in her thin hands and says in a voice that reminds me of a bird: 'So, you ran away from home. Your parents are bound to be sad.' We both shrug our shoulders. And that's the most honest answer we can give because who knows if they will miss us or not. Perhaps their sorrow will bring them together and they'll get married. My mother will stop drinking and Max's father will start talking. They'll have red-cheeked twins and move to the country where they start a home for severely-handicapped children. Anything is possible.

Suddenly the woman's face becomes blurred and Max and I are unbelievably tired. We've barely slept, the first night in the lorry doesn't really count. And for the first time I notice how tiring it is running away from home. You really can't do it every day.

Max's eyes are closing too. Where are the couple's children? I feel very heavy – and then it is dark.

* Pirogi are the type of Polish stuffed pasta, like tortellini

MAX   What a mess.

I wake up in a room that's like a complete pigsty. This is not the sort of place you put guests! Wooden walls, a tiny attic window, two beds and spiders' webs everywhere. Old toys are lying around on the floor. It looks just like a scene from a horror film, if only I'd ever seen one. Anna is lying on the other bed. I'm a bit relieved that she's still here but before I can say anything to her, the door opens with a creak – what else – and the fat man comes in.

He stares at us silently. I'm so confused that I have no idea if I'm afraid or not. The man begins to talk. He tells us that his children have gone away and that is why he and his wife are very sad. That's when he got the idea of fetching new children for her. It's a large farm, there is a lot of work to be done and his wife is mainly on her own. There's no way of escaping because there are no neighbours and only one road. And if we did sneak off then we'd enter the wood and in the wood are animals that we might prefer not to bump into. Because we ran away from home, he is assuming that we were probably not particularly happy there, so there's no reason for us not to stay. We'd get lots to eat and he would be our father and his wife our mother.

I look at the man. He's sweating. He is obviously not quite right in the head. Luckily I know I can rely on Anna. She won't say or do the wrong thing. You have to be very careful with psychopaths. They get angry if you haul them out of their own world. What a ridiculous situation. A disgusting attic, a Polish madman, winter outside and two children pretending to be adults.

Anna says that'd be fine by us, we could take to it here. Before she can say anything else, the man mutters:

'At least call me father.'

'Yes, father,' says Anna.

'Yes, father,' say I.

The man wipes his brow with a handkerchief and growls: 'So. So so so. That's all sorted then.'

During this his wife appears behind him. What on earth brought these two together? Strange that I think about that now but the two of them really don't look as if they belong together. I look around the room because I can't bear the unpleasant way the woman is looking at me – and I can't see our bags. Shit.

'Aha, so you two want to stay?' she establishes. Her voice sounds as if someone has just injured her.

Anna says: 'Yes, I don't see why not. We weren't heading for anywhere in particular.'

The woman stares mistrustfully. Then she says to Anna: 'Well, come along with me then.'

Anna gets up and follows the woman. Like me she's slept in her clothes. I stay behind with the fat man. In truth I feel like howling, but what good is that going to do?

ANNA   Did I ever tell you how we were held prisoner by psychopaths?

It's curious if things happen to you that you only know from books and films. They don't seem real somehow. I could just as easily be in a space-ship, nothing else would surprise me. Perhaps this is what happens if you enter a war zone or are captured by a murderer. Whoa, I don't want to tempt fate. In any case you feel so apathetic and so resigned. I can't think clearly, I feel as if I've been run over by a steamroller.

I trot behind the woman and study her back, even from behind there's something repellent about the way she looks. She has such a painful way of walking, as if all the cares of the world are on her shoulders.

Even at supper I thought there was something very odd about the two of them. Something's not quite right there, I thought, but that was as far as the thinking went. Sometimes you sit in the middle of an unpleasant situation and know you just have to get through it. There is no running away. We'll just have to wait and see what happens. Although I have to say I have no intention of remaining in some revolting house in Poland. I could just have easily remained in my revolting house in East Germany.

By the way, the first thing that people from friendly foreign countries (i.e. those countries East Germans are allowed to visit) ask is: West Germany or East Germany? And when you reply proudly 'East' and expect some sort of wildly enthusiastic scenes of welcome, well you could not be more wrong, old boy!! They're not even interested in your Eastern currency because they've got plenty of that themselves. Despite the fact that the GDR could almost be called a paradise compared to what I've seen around here. Well up to this point anyway. Poland is completely desolate. Here it looks as if the war only ended yesterday.

I must tell you as well that I'm astonished to find myself chattering away merrily while I follow some totally mental child murderess through her cold and relatively dark house. Yes, my dears of the future. I have ever so slightly surprised myself. I'm beginning to think we're just as cunning as that couple. We've got to let things settle down a bit, we have to find out where our things are, and then off we'll go into the oh-so-very-dangerous wood.

The woman crosses the yard with me. At first she has her bony hand on my shoulder, now she's let go. A good sign. She walks with me into a shed, there's a couple of cows standing around, and orders me to muck out and feed the cows. She leaves me standing there and I hear her bolt the shed door. Well she is a funny thing: where am I supposed to put the cow muck now?

If the good woman thinks she can shock me with actions like that, then she is way off beam. Part of our curriculum is ESP (Elementary Socialist Production) – oh how they love shortening everything in the East – and so we often spent time on an APC (Agricultural Production Co-operative). I milked the cows, mucked them out, fed them – and I love them. Cows always smell so good, and besides, their warm stupidity is comforting. When I'm with cows I can forget about everything else that is going on. Maybe I'll own a cow farm in Italy. Does Italy even have cows? And besides, the place I really want to go is Holland – I just didn't want to put Max off his stride. I've got as much of a clue about Italy as I have about Brazil.

I grab a wheelbarrow, a pitchfork, muck out the stall and barrow the stuff over to a pile in the corner. Usually you take it outside but shrewd Magda (that's her name, I heard the man calling her) has locked me in. I distribute the food mixture and water and talk to the cows about aliens and begin to feel hungry.

As soon as I think the word 'hungry' the door opens. Magda casts a glance round, says 'Good, come with me,' and we trundle across the yard back into the house and into the kitchen where there's soup. And Max. There's no sign of the fat man. I use the silence to make up newspaper headlines: '3567 Days Hard Labour in Captivity: Kidnapped as a Child, Released as an Old Woman'. I envisage being freed by a commando troop and then becoming an honorary citizen of Poland. Although that's not my heart's desire. But perhaps you can swap honorary citizenships. Two Polish for an Italian and a Dutch. Then it's heads or tails and I win the Dutch. And get a little house by a little canal.

Max is completely covered in dust. We don't talk to each other, the atmosphere just isn't right. At one end of the table Magda sits in silence, the clock ticks very loudly and a saucepan lid rattles.

MAX   I've not seen our things.

I tidied up the cellar. That was really hard work. It's not that I'm afraid of the cellar, I don't mind spiders really and I'm not afraid of the dark. Yup, you could say I was a sort of hero. And that's why I was so amazingly popular back home.

What I wanted to say was: when I was clearing out the cellar I became aware that I really am a policeman's son and that untidiness gets on my nerves. Down there everything was in a mess, supplies and wine piled up next to old junk. But there was no sign of kidnapped children, skeletons or anything like that. I think our kidnappers must be snatching children as a hobby. They haven't had a lot of practice, you can tell that by the way they're so clumsy. God only knows what got into them. Maybe they did have children and social services took them away. Or they never had any and that's why they're in crisis at the moment.

Adults are usually completely uptight because they don't recognise their own problems. Something gnaws away at them but they don't talk about it and so their problems come out in weird ways. I don't think these two are particularly evil, they're simply not particularly cunning. They didn't have much of a plan apart from: hey, let's kidnap these two children.

So I cleared out the cellar and whilst doing so I had enough time to think about how we might get away from here. First of all I have to find out where our things are. Then I've got to arrange a time with Anna. And then we'll be off.

After we'd finished eating, I suddenly remember the story of Hansel and Gretel. So I ask the woman what she plans to do with us. She looks at me terrified and replies: 'You'll remain here.'

This confirms my suspicion that they really haven't given it much thought. The man probably acted on impulse. Or he got carried away with the idea because his wife was getting thinner and thinner and more and more unhappy and he had to do something. We don't talk about it further. I go back to my cellar, Anna to her shed.

It's all very odd. But sadly less exciting than if it had happened to someone else and they told us all about it afterwards.

ANNA These are the most ridiculous kidnappers I know, did I tell you that?

I have read too many books about evil people to allow myself to be frightened by these two here.

I go back to cleaning out the cowshed. Magda has left the door open. They really have no idea. I almost want to tell her what a real kidnap would like, i.e. solitary confinement, being tied up, spotlights and talking in whispers. The pair of them could at least wear a mask. Personally I think it'd be good if they both wore bear costumes and hopped around like bunnies the whole time. Okay, I know there's something slightly off about that last idea.

I carry the muck out to the muck pile. At the same time I can inspect the outlying area. They were not lying. There is no other house in sight, only woods. But we didn't travel for an eternity down the lane, only for half an hour. At worst that's about three hours on foot, although we'll have to take care they don't follow us.

This might sound bonkers, but I don't actually mind if we stay a few more days here. I like cows, the food is great, I quite like the woods too and I can't really blame our hosts if they're a bit freaky. Life probably hasn't been too kind to them. But I have a feeling Max will want to make a quick get away. He's a boy and they don't really like being told what to do.

The only strange thing is that I miss Max out here in the cowshed. It's very odd because we've hardly spent a huge amount of time together. But I miss him. He's doing something over there in the house and that's too far away for me. I like to have him near me. And how embarrassing is that?

MAX The evening is familial, pleasant and mind-numbing.

We sit round the table together like some sort of caricature of a funny, international family. The fat man is back from his travels and yet again there's a hot supper: peas and fish fingers. That woman really knows how to bring children to their knees. I've got to get out of here quickly, another couple of days and I'll look like the fat man. The two watch us silently as we eat. Great, just how I like mealtimes, being observed like a zoo animal.

After we've finished the last fish finger, Magda asks us how we like it there and we are clever enough not to yell 'FANTASTIC' immediately. She's not stupid. So we wait a moment and then Anna replies, 'I suppose we'll get used to it.' That was very diplomatic. After the meal the fat man makes us go with him. He takes us back to the room we woke up in this morning. It's as awful as before.

The fat man turns the light out. We hear him turn the key in the lock and then lie there a bit before we start talking to each other, very quietly. The bed is lovely and soft and Anna's voice so pleasant that I completely forget we're being held prisoner. I fall asleep very quickly.

ANNA   Did I ever tell you how I just lie there and can't sleep?

I listen to Max sleeping. It makes me feel light and happy to hear him breathing. I almost think: it doesn't matter where we are, the main thing is we're together. This is what it must be like to have a brother. Except you don't have to choose a brother.

Although you couldn't really say that I chose Max, it just happened. You mustn't tell anyone, but what I'd really like is to lie in a bed next to him. We'd use the cover to make a cave and then sit under it with a torch sketching out what life will be like in Italy. Maybe other children have been here too and made a complete fuss: help, we've been kidnapped and all that. I think the reason we're not cracking up is because we've both read so much. Now I understand what it's good for.

Outside I hear owls hooting and the sounds that pine trees make when the wind blows. It smells slightly of cow and the feather duvet is incredibly warm.

But we mustn't let ourselves be taken in. Either there'll come a point when we mean nothing to them, which is not good, or they'll realise that we can report them to the police once we get away from here, and that won't be good either. The secret is to wait for the right moment to go. They have to become careless but not be at the point where they've started to think.

As I was watching the two of them at supper tonight I felt sorry for them somehow. I've no idea what it must feel like to be old and feel you've made a mess of life. I mean, there is no re-run, no opportunity to do it all again only better. I think that's the awful thing about life: that you have to try to do everything, and I mean everything, right.

MAX A brand-new shindy day and two weirdo adults.

A new day and everything is as before. The fat man arrives, opens the door, stands there silently and looks into the bedroom in embarrassment. I'd be embarrassed too. I mean, is it possible for a psychopath to hold a civilised conversation with his kidnapped victims? Some kind of everyday chit-chat? Hello there, and what glorious weather we're having, perfect for being held prisoner...?

We get dressed and Anna asks where we could wash. Even though I'm a boy and it's a well-known fact that boys like dirt, you could say even need dirt, I was going to ask the same question. Washing myself doesn't put me in the best of moods, but I don't like being dirty. And now, after being out and about for three days, I do feel grubby.

The fat man nods and we trot after him and into an actual bathroom. Of course it only has cold water. In front of the toilet, on the toilet seat and in front of the bath are some sort of revolting towelling mats, on the windows there are pink frilly curtains and everywhere there are straw posies. I've never understood this sort of furnishing. You've got to move everything out of the way in order to clean. But worse than that you end up staring at it all the time without being able to turn away, in the same way you sometimes stare at disabled people without wanting to.

The fat man closes the door on his way out and we stand there. At a loss. Because getting half-undressed in front of each other in the semi-darkness is one thing but getting completely undressed to wash, well that's just not on. Then Anna has another good idea: first she will turn around and face the wall, and then I will. And that's what we do.

Although I know that she's not going to cheat, it does seem odd to get right undressed and then wash. Yet at the same time it makes me feel slightly tingly, but I really don't want to think about that right now. Then it's Anna's turn. I would certainly never cheat either. But the sounds that she makes when she's taking off her clothes and washing herself are somehow exciting. I had seen Anna as a sort of sister but I don't have much experience of having a sister. Perhaps it's quite normal to feel a bit funny in these kind of situations. But as we stand there in the bathroom opposite each other, freshly washed and pink cheeked, I know one thing for sure: I don't ever want to be without Anna again. And she is the one I will protect above all else in the world.

After breakfast Anna goes back to her cows while I wash the steps, clear the kitchen and do stuff like that. I don't know if the pair of them ever really had children, they seem more timetabled for servants.

In one of the rooms off the kitchen I discover our rucksacks. Man they are so stupid! Of course I pretend not to have seen the room and carry on like a good boy. But I get the feeling there's something so wrong with these two that we definitely have to think about getting out of here. Tonight, if we can.

Anna   Did I ever tell you that I never want to leave here?

I think the cows have begun to recognise me. They murmured something that sounded just like: 'Aha, so you've finally washed yourself, you skinny biped.'

As I look into the large, heavy eyes of the animals I think, maybe Max could be my boyfriend. Now that we're clean. I looked at him over breakfast. Looked at him differently. I'd not really noticed before that he has very lovely blue eyes. And he has quite long blonde hair, despite his girl's haircut. I don't mind him being so thin. What is to stop us staying here until we're grown up? It really is very nice here, at least, the countryside is, and if we had to go home now there'd be a whole fuss. Then we'd probably not be allowed to see each other again. Each of us would have our own life and it would be a solitary one.

Better not to dwell on it.

The sun is shining today, the sky is blue, the woods are full of hoarfrost and the muck is steaming. Okay, maybe that last image doesn't fit into the whole romantic picture but anyone who's ever been on a farm will know what I mean. It's such a good feeling to be with the animals and to do physical work. I'm almost beginning to think that this is what a fulfilled life could look like: Max and I get married, the couple go into an old people's home and we continue to run the farm, renovate the place etc.

Just as I'm thinking about stripping out the bathroom and making a bonfire with the pink mats, the cowshed door is ripped open.

MAX   We've got to leave, right now.

I've got the rucksacks. Magda's just gone down to the cellar and the fat man is nowhere to be seen. It's still morning, it's going to be light for a while yet and there's no time like the present to escape.

Anna doesn't grasp what I'm on about for several minutes. She stands in the cowshed snuggling up to a cow and looking at the ceiling. Girls, really. By the time she finally gets moving, it's almost too late. I peep through a gap in the open cowshed door and see Magda running towards us in some excitement. I need an idea quick. I pull Anna behind a large container filled with dried hay. At that moment Magda yanks open the cowshed door and looks around, breathing heavily. The cows look at her complete-ly undisturbed before she turns and lollops back to the house. I think she's gone to tell the fat man. I saw a radio set in one of the rooms.

And there's not enough time to run into the woods. The farm is huge and there's time to find somewhere to hide. Anna says we should hide up in the hayloft in the cowshed. We'll be able to see clearly between the loose planks of wood and will know when the way is clear to escape. So we climb onto the platform without using the ladder and take up position, our faces pressed against two gaps in the wood. I don't think our spot would necessarily have won the Best Hiding Place Award. We wait.

Just look over there. A small Wartburg car with German number plates is pulling up, an excited man jumps out and Magda starts talking to him. A couple of minutes later the fat man's lorry drives up. He jumps out of the cabin as Magda and the man begin to argue. And then the wind changes direction or the cows stop lowing or something like that, because suddenly we get what's going on. The German wanted to pick up his new delivery yesterday and is complaining that the couple used the delivery for their own ends. And then he complains that two from the last delivery are ill and adds that he's going to inform his boss about all this.

The fat man then says that the two children can't have got very far, maybe just into the woods but the trees aren't very thick. And with regards the other two dropping out, he'll come and do a couple of hours in the factory himself. The German mutters under his breath a bit more then gets back into his Wartburg and speeds off.

We look at each other in surprise and slowly the message gets through. They're not dear old poor people. They collect children professionally. For a factory. And the guy that runs the factory has an air about him that you would not exactly describe as friendly.

Magda and the fat man go back into the house. As it starts to get dark I rouse Anna, we drop down into the cowshed and run like mad. Towards the lorry.

ANNA   Did I ever tell you how exciting our little escape is?

So we lie puffing and panting on the floor of the lorry. We've seen this in many escape-from-prison movies. There's always somebody hiding out in the laundry van.

We're ready for the off, for a little tour round the factory. And while we're there we'll do a bit of cleaning up, like Superman and Supergirl. Although I have absolutely no idea how the bandits are managing to run a factory full of stolen kids in the middle of Poland without anyone noticing. But then the Poles are good at not noticing anything.

In the GDR the Poles are the butt of everyone's jokes, they're considered the stupid people of the Eastern bloc. But nobody ever mentions the Nazis and concentration camps in Poland. Of course everyone is always banging on about the Nazis in Germany (West Germany, of course). But I've discovered that there were quite awful camps in Poland, right next to perfectly ordinary residential areas.

Now I have no idea why that idea suddenly sprung into my mind.

The sound of a car door being banged shut brought me back to the present. The lorry's engine is turned on and we set off. I look over to Max. He's hidden himself under some empty sacks and is now lifting the awning of the lorry so we can see out. Here's the lane we drove down. After a while we come to the spur road to the motorway, then we're off down a country road, through a small village, along a lane and drive up to two large barracks.

We stop. The fat man jumps out of the driver's cabin. We look at each other. Fools rush in where angels fear to tread. And we slowly climb down from the back of the lorry. In the twilight we can see the fat man running to one of the buildings. He is panting terribly, as if he might explode any second. We follow him at a suitable distance. We really are bang in the middle of a detective series.

The building is brightly lit and looks terrifying in the darkness, as if designed for terrible revelations. Scraps of clouds chase each other across the sky, behind them is a huge moon. Tentatively we look through the window. It is unbelievable. About fifty children are sorting pieces of stone on an assembly line. Probably highly-radioactive material, although the children look healthy as far as it is possible to see. However they don't seem to be having a lot of fun. Two fairly miserably blokes are running alongside the conveyor belt giving the children an occasional slap or kick up the backside. That is possibly the most humiliating thing ever. A grown up once kicked me up the backside. You're completely helpless and feel like a dog. The fat man is standing next to the entrance and talking to the German that we saw earlier. Anna and I stay completely still while we study the scene.

MAX   Shit, now we're going to have to play Robin Hood.

Anna slips round to the other building. She's completely in cops and robbers' mode, I think she thinks the children will be turned into sausage meat in there. Between you and me, what I really want to do is retreat. Courage was never one of my positive points.

Anna comes back and tells me that the other building is a dormitory. The whole thing is really incredible. If I saw this scene in a film I'd think they'd gone totally over the top. We're not living in Charles Dickens' time.

Suddenly there's a terrible sound. The smidgeon of courage I possess makes its escape. We squeal and hold onto each other. Boy, are we behaving like superheroes. But it's only a sort of siren and after a few seconds we realise what's going on: it's the end of the shift. The conveyor belt stops. The children line up. We just have enough time make it round the side of the barracks to a shed, the ideal hiding place.

We barely make it behind the shed when the door opens. The children walk out of the factory in a line and into the dormitory, with the overseers walking alongside them. We move slightly and watch the children sit down on their beds. In the meantime the German and the fat man have left the factory. The fat man sets off in his lorry, the German yells something at the overseers and then disappears in his Wartburg. So now there's us and approximately fifty children on one side and two overseers on the other. Not bad odds.

ANNA   Did I ever tell you about the poor children?

They're just sitting on their beds. Their clothes are quite shabby but seem to be clean. The two overseers distribute bread, cheese and hot tea. I think. It could be just hot water. The children look as if they've not been in a proper domestic situation for some time. They have sort of funny old faces. That must be the look children get when they have to be grown up but in actual fact are not.

After supper the two men go up and down the rows of beds and put shackles on the legs of the children. It's so peculiar that they're so lethargic and just let it happen. I mean, there's fifty children, or maybe even more. If they simply ran out of the building the two over-seers wouldn't be able to do a thing. But the children just sit there and wait patiently until they're tied up, then they keel over and apparently fall straight asleep.

The two men turn the light out and go into the next-door room. We can see into it from outside. It's a small lobby where they hang up a large bunch of keys and pour vodka into glasses, drink up and then go into the next room, where they lie down on the beds. All this without washing, well, bon appetit!

It just can't be this simple. All we have to do is take down the bunch of keys, release the children's shackles and then they'll all be free. After that we can fetch help from the village. That's it, that's what we'll do.

MAX   The great liberation campaign.

We wait for about an hour until the two men are fast asleep, then we slip through the children's dormitory into the lobby. Somehow it's all too easy. Anna grabs the bunch of keys while I stand at the door listening to the two men snore. There's no movement. We go back into the dormitory and begin to free the children. Most of them go on sleeping but one young boy wakes up and looks at us appalled.

There are a lot more boys here than girls.

We'd freed about ten children when another boy suddenly hisses at us: 'Are you mad? Go away!' I say, 'There's no need to be afraid, we'll get you out of here,' but the boy shakes his head in irritation. Perhaps they're so used to being kept prisoner that they've forgotten how to move on their own.

We'd untied about twenty children when suddenly the light goes on. The two overseers stand there motionless in the doorway. Anna begins to scream, she yells at the children who've already been freed: 'Come on, move yourselves, get out!'

And then it gets really bizarre. The light is very bright and suddenly there's all these children sitting on their beds looking at us strangely. I've no idea whether they're suffering from shock or what's going on. Then something extraordinary happens: a tall boy, much taller than me, stands up and hits me, then he takes the keys off me and says: 'Just stop all this crap. No-one asked for your help. Go away and leave us alone.'

'But you can run away,' Anna shouts at them.

The boy replies, 'And where are we supposed to run away to, you idiots? It's winter, our parents are drinkers, or no longer around, and it's not bad here. So we play the game. We pretend we've been taken prisoner, if that's what the adults want. So now go away.'

Anna and I stand there in the middle of the dormitory and cannot say a word. The two overseers begin to laugh. The children lie back down in their beds and ignore us. It is incredible. They prefer to remain imprisoned voluntarily rather than try and do something about their own lives. Unbelievable!

And how on earth are we going to get out of this situation with any dignity? No chance.

We leave the room like two dogs that have fallen into a pond. I mean, we all know what that looks like. In the doorway we look at each other. How embarrassing. That's what I'd call a Robin Hood operation gone badly wrong. Anna tries to save our honour somehow and suggests they've been drugged. Followed by: 'I know, let's go into the village and fetch help.' Well that is at least a plan. Far better that we get going instead of standing around in the doorway completely gobsmacked.

The light goes out in the dormitory. We run off. I can't say I'm exactly feeling like a man right now. Anna seems to understand, in the way that she seems to understand everything. She begins to talk.

ANNA   Did I ever tell you ...

You know, I've often felt the way I do now. As if I was the most embarrassed person in the whole world. I'll tell you something now: my mother didn't just trip and fall. She was drunk. She is permanently drunk. And each time I felt it was because of me, because I hadn't succeeded in entertaining her well enough. And now I'm going to tell you about the most embarrassing moment in my life. We never celebrated Christmas, I never knew why, maybe it was because of religious reasons. But I thought that my mother might like a Christmas if I prepared one for her. It was the 24th of December and it was snowing. I had a fairly high temperature but all the same I trotted round the town from shop to shop stealing presents for my mother. A watch, underwear, chocolates and a Father Christmas hat that I bought. I talked an old man into giving me a Christmas tree, a stunted old thing. I dragged it all the way back home, I was shaking and sweating, my temperature was in the hundreds. At home I wrapped all the presents, decorated the tree with cotton wool, put candles on it and dressed myself up as Father Christmas with a bath towel and the hat. I sat there for hours. The candles burnt down, I fetched new ones. At about midnight my mother turned up. I was so excited. She opened the door, saw me all dressed up and spotted the tree, and then said: 'For heaven's sake, don't be so embarrassing.' She was blind drunk. I nearly died in that moment. The whole joy I wanted to convey to her turned to shame. I threw the presents out of the window. I couldn't even cry because that would have reminded me that I exist.

MAX   After that we were quiet.

I can think of many situations where I wanted my father to be a friend and he demolished me in the same way. And I know exactly what she means. I begin to feel a bit better because I know that I'm not the only one who feels like a failure. The stupid thing is that as a child you don't feel like a child. You don't say to yourself: come on now, don't take it all so seriously, you're still a child. I feel how I feel. And I can tell you that that feeling is not exactly great.

Meanwhile we've reached the village. We don't hang around for long but ring the doorbell of the first house. A fat woman opens the door. She doesn't speak German so she calls her son, who is about our age. We tell him what's going on just a few metres away from his house: prisoners, child labour, returned escapees. The boy interrupts us.

'So what, we know all that. They sort pieces of stone looking out for precious metals. The whole village lives off it. Go away and mind your own business.'

The boy closes the door with a bang. And we're left standing there like idiots again. Like idiots, it must be said, at nine o'clock at night, in a Polish village whose name we don't even know. And if we did know it, it wouldn't change a thing.

ANNA Did I ever tell you how we set off towards the border?

We slink along the dark village road. A full moon is hanging behind the clouds, but there's no wolf in sight. It's odd how so many people allow themselves be imprisoned. Sometimes properly, like the children, but mainly in boring professions that they don't like. Then they go home every evening and go to bed early because they're afraid they'll be tired in the morning and that'll make the job more unbearable.

I've seen many people who lead the sort of life they never really wanted. They slipped into it and are then too tired to think up another life. I don't know even if it can work out any other way. Or if running away is the solution.

There are some adults who seem to have a wonderful life, artists, theatre directors and the like. But those lives are only for the very few and certainly not for me. I remember occasions when I was in the apartments of people like that. Even though I was quite young, I understood that those were good lives, lives with books, wooden floors and without fear.

I think you've got to make a real effort for your life. You can't neglect it otherwise you give up and wake up in a prison. At some point or another my mother stopped paying attention. I think she chose the easiest solution: she separated from my father, because she thought that would bring her back to life. But I don't think it's that simple, I don't think that another person is responsible for one's life.

And while I'm thinking all this, I notice that my thoughts have come to their own border. I have the feeling that I know something, but I can't grab hold of it. It flutters away. I hope that will wear off when I'm older.

MAX   Bored – for the first time.

After we've been walking for an hour or maybe a hundred hours, we arrive at a sign that says – if I understand this right – that it's another twenty kilometres to the border.

Somehow we've run out of breath. We walk down the country road falteringly like little robots, well, little unspectacular Eastern bloc robots with nasty anoraks. And there's no real country charm to cheer us up so we can recite poems or maybe spontaneously burst into song. It is grey, dark and cold. There are trees, fields and the sweet-rose bower is dead.

You often hear adults say: we get on so well we don't have to say a word. That's bloody obvious. If all's going well then everyone can keep their mouth shut. It's not something that requires a medal. But when you're frozen through and demoralised and don't know where you're going or what your future might hold, then the silence thing looks different.

I feel no connection to Anna, and none to myself. Everything is miserable and boring. I try to run a film in my thoughts but I just can't think up any stories with beautiful actresses. Maybe it's because I'm feeling so small and insignificant so I quite understand that no actress would be leaping up and down to bump into me right now.

Instead I'd be quite happy to run through the film of my life as apparently happens when people die. However sadly there isn't much life to run. Remembering my first day at school will hardly have them stamping and cheering.

So what happens to an old person who, let's say, is eighty and as they lie dying, realise that there was nothing in their life worth remembering ? Might they not kill a geriatric nurse in the last few hours before death, so that at least there was something?

So there you have it, the sum total of everything that occurred to me as entertainment. Not much to show for half an hour's walk.

ANNA   Did I ever tell you that escaping can be boring?

I start to count my steps out of sheer despair. But after three hundred even that gets boring as hell.

Children often get bored. But then they don't just think, boy am I bored. Instead they begin to cause a fuss, to howl or to rip the furniture apart. I was always bored witless when I had to sit in bars with my mother. Now there's a cue to remember my mother and spend a few minutes thinking about her. But I don't want to do that just now. By the time I've finished I'll feel melancholic.

Max is icily silent and staring ahead. This is the first time that I really have to make an effort to find something to say to him. I have that with other people all the time, not knowing what I should say. But this is the first time it has happened with Max. I hope that this low point of our relationship will pass quickly.

If I had more life experience I'd probably say: 'Come on, the pair of you have just been victims of a kidnap; you've visited imprisoned children and you've not eaten anything for ages, it's completely normal for your mood to sink so low.' But I'm worried that the good feeling between us was only imagined. I've mentioned already, I think, that I feel more alone when I'm with people than when I'm on my own. If this happens with Max, then it'll be totally awful. And what's more, we're in a strange country.

I've no idea how long we dragged ourselves through the night, probably hours. And then suddenly a car appears. It phut-phuts slowly but surely towards us. And stops. Unbelievable. An old woman looks out of the window. She has a nice face. And speaks not a word of German. On a map she shows us that she has to cross exactly that bit of Czechoslovakia that we too have to pass through before going on through Hungary, Romania, and finally to Bulgaria, where we'll board a ship to take us to Turkey or cross the straits to Italy. It all seems quite simple, don't you think?

MAX   How comfortable.

Lovely to be in a car like this. We sit in the back. The heating is on and there's classical music on the radio. It's just right for tonight. It makes everything feel so friendly that you immediately understand how film music works. Take any old boring image (Russians, sitting alone in their cold apartments), put sad music underneath and suddenly the whole story is very deep.

The woman, whose car we get into, seems to be really peaceful. I'd say she was a granny but then you have to be really careful about that as a child. She might only be forty and then they really don't want to be viewed as grandmas. The woman smells of cookies and looks just like the mother I would love to have had. Everything about her is clean and pink and smells lovely. Plus she begins to stuff us all with all sorts of things, biscuits and tea and apples. We stay silent as we chew away. The grandmother hums quietly.

After a while Anna's head slips onto my shoulder. I think she's nearly asleep. I can't see her because it's fairly dark in the car. There's only a weak light coming from the instrument panel. Her head is quite light. Her hair tickles my nose a bit. I push my hand under her head and for a moment I'm so ridiculously happy that it's embarrassing. Perhaps I should try sleeping for a bit too.

ANNA   Did I ever tell you that I'm in a very odd mood?

It's night outside. And I sink more and more into myself and freeze, because it's not that great in there either. You have to fight this sort of thing. And so I begin to talk quietly.

MAX   Anna talks.

I sometimes have the feeling that life is very uncertain. It feels like I'm standing on a raft and if I took one step either way it would start to roll. Or like everything could suddenly be pulled from under me and I'd fall into a bottomless pit. I forget this feeling usually when my life follows a very strict routine. When I go to school, come home, eat, read and then sleep. When there's no routine, then uncertainty appears in its place. Because then there's nothing I can hang onto. You are here, and that's good, but I think that you share these feelings. And two people standing on a raft doesn't make it any more stable.

Is what Anna said. And then she fell asleep.

ANNA   Did I ever tell you how it was when I woke up?

Here we go again, I think to myself, waking up and hanging around some sort of car park — I wake up and I crawl out of the car and find myself in front of a sweet little house. (A witch's house? Hansel and Gretel?) It looks like a nice day, almost spring-like. The sun is shining, and if the birds hadn't all been unemployed and so emigrated to farms where they breed bog-rats, then they most certainly would have been singing.

We are standing on a narrow village street. The car has pulled up in front of a small wooden-framed house and the woman is inviting us in. After our previous experience we really should run away screaming right now, but I don't have any sense of danger. The inside of the small house is like a doll's house. It is warm and smells nice, everything is clean and cosy. The woman makes it clear that we can bathe and rest before we continue with our journey. Beforehand it would never have occurred to me to get into strangers' baths, but as a rebel you can't afford to be shy. It doesn't matter what was before.

And you should have seen me lying in the bathtub filled with bubble bath. Astonishing. After bathing for about an hour – and I have to say at this point that bathing here is pure luxury, there is a constant supply of hot water, you can re-fill the bath, the bathroom is heated, there are fluffy towels and so on – I wrap myself up in a bath towel the woman put out for me and wander down the corridor. In the living room next to the chimney there is a huge sofa with snug covers placed on it. I wrap myself up in one of them and fall asleep straightaway.

When I wake up, the woman, Max and a boy in a wheelchair are all sitting at the table. They're eating cakes and drinking hot tea. It's like being in paradise. I join them. It's marble cake, black and white and fresh. The boy sitting at the table is called Igor and speaks some German. And is very good-looking. The sort of good-looking that gives you a shock and makes your mouth drop open. He's got black hair and very light-coloured green eyes. It can't be simple for a boy to be so exaggeratedly beautiful. Who is ever going to take him seriously?

He translates for his mother some of what we tell him, and she murmurs continuously: Holy Mary Mother of God. Which is roughly the equivalent of: well I never. (For future generations: officially God does not exist in the GDR and Eastern bloc countries. There are churches and occasional services, but hardly anyone goes apart from young people, who do it as a form of rebellion. Otherwise religions, all of them, are viewed as a means of suppressing the people.)

Suddenly the woman springs up and leaves the house. Igor explains that his mother can't bear to see children suffer. She's going to see if she can find someone to drive us through Hungary or at least as far as Budapest.

And then something happens. It's like I've suddenly been hypnotised. I just stare at Igor. I've no idea what we are talking about but I find everything he says totally fascinating. I get the feeling that I've never enjoyed myself so much with anyone before.

MAX He is talking complete codswallop, unbelievable.

Anna has completely forgotten me. She's virtually crawled into the mouth of that show-off. Igor had an accident. Five years ago he was run over by a lorry in front of the house. They told him he'd probably never walk again because there was a defect in his head. Igor felt he'd come to terms with it. Even before the accident he hated sports (how cool) and preferred to read (ditto ditto). Besides, he can still visit his favourite spot in his wheelchair and he'd like to show it to Anna. Just great.

I feel like a lump of shit. Completely superfluous to requirement. I'm furious and sad and have no idea what's wrong. Up until now we've been a single unit, Anna and I. Us against the rest of the world. And suddenly she leaves me sitting here at the table as if I don't exist. I've no idea what to do next. I mean, I've not got a room to go to. Or any other sort of place that's mine.

ANNA   Did I ever tell you about Igor?

At some stage I look over to Max. He's sitting in the corner concentrating very hard on a book. Too hard, if you ask me. I have a bit of a bad conscience, but I'm far to wound up to talk to him normally right now. And soon as I look away from Max I sink right into Igor. He's so funny. And the way his hair falls across his eyes, it just looks lovely.

Later on his mother comes back laden with food. She tells us that we can travel to Budapest tomorrow with friends, or, if we wanted, we could spend a couple more days with them, to rest up. That night Max and I have our first real row.

Max   Trust no-one.

How they sit together and throw their heads back when they laugh. And how they laugh. And Anna swings her legs and is all friendly. Ideally I'd like to shoot Igor. Or at least make a doggy meal out of him.

He's a successful combination of clever dick and handsome boy. I accept that the whole accident thing was pretty bad but it doesn't excuse everything. The way he talks with his head at an angle so that his hair falls across his eyes nicely and he can brush it away carelessly. Then there's his gentle voice and that oh so sweet sounding Czech accent. It must be put on. He ignores me completely and has eyes only for Anna. And she is stuck to him like a leech. Girls are so stupid. Suddenly I'm in a really bad mood.

After supper we're led to a great big double bed. Well thanks a bunch! Yesterday I'd have found that very exciting and been so happy. But today all I can think is: bugger, how embarrassing. We get undressed silently, with our backs to each other. And then nip under the covers.

Anna is wriggling around non-stop — she's completely overwrought. I ask her, mainly as a matter of form, if she'd like to stay on for a couple of days. And she replies, 'Oh yes, that'd be great.'

At first I'm so shocked I can't move: she's giving up our friendship for some idiot with black hair she only met a couple of hours ago. There is of course the fact that Igor is already fourteen. A proper adult. I get so livid that I throw myself on the bed and push my face into the pillow so that I don't weep with anger. That'd be the final straw.

At last Anna asks, 'Is everything alright?'

And that somehow releases a rage in me and I yell at her for a while. When I can't think of anything else to say, Anna says. 'If that's the case and you do think I'm a stupid idiotic girl, then it's best we go our separate ways.'

And after that neither of us says a thing. I lie there for hours wide-awake. I'm furious and in complete despair. It's quite obvious that there's no going back. I'm going to have to continue hitchhiking solo. And that makes me feel unhappier than I have ever felt in my entire life.

ANNA   Did I ever tell you how I split up with Max?

I lie in bed, pressed close to Max, and can't get to sleep. Everything's so confusing and so stupid. How quickly everything can fall apart. It only takes a couple of sentences. I don't recognise myself any more. Well, that's what people say. As if I have any idea who I am at my age.

In any case, the whole afternoon I was completely beside myself. Nothing like that has ever happened before. I could have spent the whole night sitting next to Igor and talking. Or not talking, just looking at him. Oh I don't know. I'm completely away with the fairies.

I've totally forgotten Max. That's right, I admit it: I don't care whether he stays or carries on alone as long as I can stay here. I don't want to leave, that's for sure. I don't want to think about tomorrow or next month. I just want to wake up in the morning and see Igor.

What was that thought just now?

Max is not asleep either. He lies next to me and I have a feeling he wants to cry. But I don't want to comfort him. At this moment I just want him to go away.

A yellow full moon is shining into the room but of course there are no dogs howling. Just at those times when they should be howling, they decide especially not to. I listen to Max being wide-awake and can't think of anything to say. Luckily at some stage I fall asleep.

MAX   I am out of here.

As soon as I'm certain Anna is asleep, I get dressed quietly and leave the house. I don't trip over, the stairs don't creak and the door doesn't bang behind me. That's usually what happens and then everyone comes running and persuades you not to go. But this time nothing goes wrong, no one comes running and so I go. I don't really want to leave this warm house in the middle of the night. But there are some things that a man's just gotta do. And I can't stay there and watch Anna lapping up Igor's winning smile. Just not possible.

Outside there's a fat full moon and it's almost as bright as in daytime. I walk along the empty village road with no idea where I'm going. Just away from weird Anna, beautiful Igor and more humiliation. Aha, now I have the word for the feeling: I feel humiliated. Suddenly, without wanting to, I seem to have become Anna's little brother. Whereas in fact I always felt more like … well like what? … I know, more like her friend. I didn't feel like a child, but like a person that together with another person was doing something grown-up. I'm not really sure exactly why I'm so livid, but I am. I could rip a stupid bear to pieces. Apropos: are there any bears round here? And what do they do at night?

After walking for half an hour I've got my rhythm. I'm no longer yearning to go back to bed but feel just like a machine. If needs must, then I'll walk across the whole of stupid Czechoslovakia.

ANNA   Did I ever tell you how messed up I am?

When I wake up Max is not next to me. He's bound to be in the bathroom. But the bathroom is empty and when I come back there's no Max to be seen. And then I notice his rucksack has disappeared as well.

I fall onto the bed as if someone has kicked me in the back of my knees. What have I gone and done? I am completely revolted by myself and ideally would like to run away from myself. I see myself flirting and giggling with Igor and how Max was sitting there in the corner. I imagine the situation the other way round and could kill myself with disgust. So now I'm hanging around in the grottiest backwater in Czechoslovakia, something in all honesty I have never been able to say before and … what did I want to say? No idea. I go down into the kitchen. Igor's mother is standing there as if she belongs. For some people it's totally obvious where they belong. I am someone, on the other hand, who looks out of place everywhere.

I sit down at the table. The woman says something in Czech and then places eggs, bacon, bread and a malted drink in front of me. It sits there, the food, looking at me. I don't think I will ever be able to eat anything ever again. A couple of minutes later Igor rolls into the kitchen. And now I'm one hundred percent confused. Suddenly my ribcage is in knots, my heart beats faster and I get sweaty palms. How embarrassing. And then I go and forget that I'll never eat again, my complete confusion about Max and that I don't know how I'm ever to find him again – in fact, I forget everything.

I look at Igor. He's glowing. I get the feeling I've never seen anything quite so beautiful before. He's heavenly, proportionate and perfect. I have to admit that his disability as well as his appearance makes him interesting. There's something exotic about it. I know I shouldn't be thinking that. But it's the truth, and I do try to always think the truth.

Igor beams at me and I forget the rest of my life: that I'm a child who's run away from home, that I don't know where and how to grow up, that it's winter. I grin at Igor like an idiot and notice that my face is almost grimacing. Soon we're sitting next to each other and talking while we dive into breakfast. No, the truth is that Igor is talking and stuffing his face. I'm listening, giggling ridiculously and eating nothing.

Igor talks, about everything. About life in Czechoslovakia, how it's similar to life in the GDR: i.e. there's nothing to buy, no travel, no fun. Igor's mother I think is just happy that her son is happy. She leaves us alone in the kitchen with biscuits and cocoa and disappears.

At some stage Igor asks me if I'd like to see his favourite spot. The way I feel is that I want to do everything he wants to do. I'd even visit a military parade ground or a lime pit. So we go outside. I think my face is quite pink. Besides I can't get a single sensible sentence out. The only thing I can think is that it's wonderful to walk down the road alongside Igor. After a while we turn off onto a small road through the woods. The frozen ground crunches underneath the wheelchair wheels and I begin to feel all romantic. Then we're there, at Igor's favourite spot. It's a small pond with weeping willows. Everything is covered in a layer of ice. It looks like the garden of an English country house. That's something I do know about, I have read *Wuthering Heights* after all.

Igor looks into the distant horizon and says, 'Since my accident I come here a lot. The place is timeless and I feel so light among all this nature, light enough to be able to walk again. Or light enough that it doesn't matter if I walk again or not. Do you know what I mean?'

Of course I know what he means.

'Come here, sit down.' Igor says.

I look at him baffled. He pats his knee and without thinking much about it, I sit down. Okay, we're sitting together in his chair on the edge of a pond and I have no idea what to do next. But that doesn't matter because Igor takes hold of my head and begins to kiss me. So this is it, I begin to think, and then I don't think any more and am only – outside myself? I don't know. I don't find the kissing to be so great. Somehow it's very peculiar to have a strange face so close to your own.

Besides, I'm really aware that I'm sitting on a boy, well on his lap, even though I don't know him. In books (and I'm thinking here of *Wuthering Heights* again) people always forget themselves when they kiss, or are carried away by waves. I'm not. I just feel slightly sick. I'd prefer to be slightly further away from Igor. So that I can see him, see his eyes and his beautiful hair. Oh, whatever. Let's just go with the kissing. I try to close my eyes and give in totally, as described in the books. But I find it embarrassing. And then Igor grabs hold of me. Well, hold of where my breasts would be if only I had breasts. And that really is just too much.

After about half an hour I start to get cold and begin to shiver so violently that Igor notices, 'Come on, let's go back,' he says. And I climb down gladly. On the way back we're fairly quiet. Back in the house I go up to the room where I slept last night and lie down on the bed to think about it all.

MAX   In a foul mood.

I wandered through the night, completely empty with rage, and then I happened upon a sort of shed by the side of the road. I know it doesn't sound that crazy because people are always finding sheds that they can hide in or burn down. Or make a delicious doggy recipe. However this shed was open and inside there was straw and wood. Now that's what I call a proper shed!

I don't know if I slept longer than half an hour at a stretch. I was sad and angry and I had run out of plans. The idea of running away together was never-ending. I could imagine everything as a pair. But on my own? It is not at all funny. I felt very lonely that night and then of course I hear a screech owl. Old wives have it that you will live as many years as the owl screeches. I stopped counting at twenty but the owl didn't open his mouth much more after that.

When morning arrived I could have wept, because I so did not want to keep on running. But I did, and after about quarter of an hour a lorry stopped. And that's where I'm sitting now.

And I can't be bothered with anything. Outside Eastern bloc crap is whizzing past, misery in the country. Houses that look as if we are still at war. Heavens it's so miserable. How can people go on living?

Unhindered we cross into Hungary. It looks exactly the same here. I had some images in my mind of a puszta,* trickling streams and horses. That'd be nice. Instead there's low houses, old barracks and dogs. Loads and loads of freezing dogs.

I'm gradually becoming an expert in lorry travel, so I sit in silence. The driver is also the silent type. He leaves me alone, which is great, so I can sit next to him and be unhappy.

We're heading for Budapest. Don't ask why. Perhaps everyone should hitch to Budapest once in their life. And maybe when I'm there I'll get on a train and go home. Then there's bound to be trouble and I'll have to spend a few more years living with my father. And then what? Then I'll start some sort of socialist study, maybe medicine if I can get in, but I stand a good chance being a policeman's son. Only three people from every class is allowed to go to the EOS, a sort of extended grammar school, to do school leaving exams. More important than the actual marks you get is whether you're a farmer's son or a worker's son or not. To be the child of intellectuals is not

163

good at all. The only chance they have is to go into the army for three years beforehand. But nobody wants to do that apart from a few complete idiots. There are two of them in our class. Proper clever-clogs. They're not particularly cunning, just loud and know it all. I've no idea how they feel or if they feel anything at all.

There are people who appear to be impregnable because they have such a coarse soul. Or because they don't think too much. I'm always astonished that such people can be satisfied without ever asking any questions. They're the ones who say: the GDR is a great country, I love learning, I do sports and I'm proud of my parents and the Party. And they mean it, they really do. That makes them untouchable, so superior. People who grovel on the other hand are easy to hurt, because they are so brittle on the outside.

So why am I thinking about school just now? Perhaps because I'm gradually trying to get used to the idea of going back. Mission failed. Here he comes crawling back, the one who ran away, his tail between his legs. I really must not let myself think about it.

Here we go: new thought. Budapest. I've got two hundred marks in my pocket. I can use them to stay somewhere overnight, in fact over several nights – as long as people do rent rooms out to children. Besides, the day after tomorrow

I'll be fourteen. On my own. In a room that I'm not sure anyone is going to let me have. It's enough to make you weep.

And so we drive along the unbelievably boring Hungarian roads. The driver is lost in his own thoughts. And I'm a failure.

* A Hungarian steppe.

ANNA   Did I ever tell you that I'm not sure about anything?

After about two hours on my – what do I mean my! I mean on THE bed – I still don't feel any better. I feel as if something has happened that I didn't want to happen.

I don't know.

I would have liked to have gone walking with Igor forever and talking to him. Dreaming about boys is one thing but actually being with them is quite another. When it comes to touching and kissing boys then I can state categorically that it's just not my thing. I don't really want to be that hands on, with all the spit and everything. It's just too much.

At some stage it gets dark. This awful feeling is still there but it's getting weaker and so I start to think there might be some sort of future for Igor and myself. He is so beautiful. And funny. Perhaps we'll simply stay together and grow together, until we marry. I know that sounds extremely naïve, but that is precisely what I am thinking. I picture myself walking along next to him, then sitting down somewhere, his hair falls over his eyes and we talk. Then he takes hold of my hands. Bizarrely, the thought of him taking hold of my hands is more exciting than the reality of kissing.

I'm still lying on the bed, I must have been here for hours. Outside it's getting dark and my feelings return. I feel a bit nervous and I've almost forgotten the unpleasant thoughts. Perhaps the beginning of a lifelong love affair is always tricky.

I just can't bear to think that I've upset Max because of a mistake.

A while later and Igor's mother calls me down to eat. I go down to join her feeling a bit uptight. I feel ashamed but I have no idea why. Then Igor comes rolling in and it's as if nothing has happened. He talks and tells jokes while eating the dumplings his mother made, and I sit next to him, look at him and think about Max. What is he doing just now? He is much more awkward and less self-confident than Igor. In reality I'm more like Max and closer to him than to this wonderfully handsome boy.

Besides, I've got a funny idea that he's not really interested in me.

MAX   Budapest is good to me.

The lorry driver lets me out in the centre of Budapest and I like it straightaway. There are places that make you feel better at once. Like being with a completely trustworthy person.

Budapest is how I imagine the West to be. Loads of coffee houses and bright shops, good-looking people on the streets, tiny alleys, a wide river and huge old buildings. I walk around for a while and think: the city and I must share the same star sign. Or: I must have been a Hungarian in my last life. I stand on a bridge and look down at the Danube flowing under other bridges, there must be a couple of dozen of them, and suddenly I feel impelled to show it all to Anna. I push the thought aside as it hurts too much and hurry away. Away from thoughts of my humiliation. Through beautiful narrow streets and onto a hilltop. At the top is a castle and you can look down over the whole city and there are souvenir shops everywhere. There is even a youth hostel.

Cool! I'm a youth and I need a hostel. And who is going to tell me how old I am? The day after tomorrow I'll be fourteen, but in case I've not mentioned it: I could pass as a young-looking fifteen-year old. I take a deep breath and walk into a building that is at least 7,000 years old and has stone floors, vaulted ceilings and crystal chandeliers. Everything is very chic. I on the other hand feel like a complete failure.

The absolute worst thing about being a child is that you feel so unsure. I do believe that this gradually disappears – with a bit of luck or a reasonable life. There are grown-ups who appear not to feel as if they are constantly being watched or think that everything they say is stupid. I have both these feelings fairly often and they are very strong. Some children and teenagers on the other hand seem to be quite self-confident, but they usually either have parents as teachers or are stupid.

I try to count backwards to pull myself together. I read that once. It has zero effect. So I walk up to the reception desk. There's an old woman sitting there who doesn't even look at me properly and who – hello comrade of the East – speaks Russian. Without any difficulty I get a bed in a twin room. And there's no other guest as yet, says the old woman.

Me and my extraordinary international language skills. Six lessons of Russian a week, but only one of English. Really one should be able to speak all the languages of the world. Preferably without having to learn them.

I stride up the stairs in a manly fashion with a completely new sense of being adult. For the very first time I will be alone in a hotel bedroom. Well, at least in something very similar. The room is nice, white and clean. There is check-patterned bed linen and even a washbasin, and what is more, the view out of the window is the best you could possibly picture. Budapest at dusk. I hope that the other bed will remain empty. Perhaps I'm in luck, who is mad enough to travel in winter?

I set off out to buy bread, cheese and lemonade and come back and sit in my room. I'm beginning to feel a bit better. Tonight I will sleep, that much is sure.

ANNA   Did I ever tell you how I made a complete fool of myself?

The cold Czech moon is shining into the room. It looks so porous, like a bone. A twig knocks against the window and I toss and turn in the bed. I'm beside myself. I keep on seeing Igor before my eyes. Did I ever tell you what he looked like? Well, I might be in danger of repeating myself but I will mention it anyway: his face is like a cat's, with strong cheekbones and large, slightly slanting eyes. His hair is fairly long and falls in curls onto his shoulders. He's slim but with really broad shoulders and strong arms, probably because of the wheelchair. And he seems to know just about everything.

After supper he talked about the Prague Spring. I'd never heard about it. It was in 1968 and Czechoslovakia was in the process of changing. Not turning to capitalism but more like a very modern version of socialism.

(Note to the following generations: in capitalism, money is all-powerful. Anyone who has enough money can do what they like: for example sell all sorts of things in a shop, get rich from it and then buy cars, houses, ships and everything else. Capitalism is all about consumption: everything has to be more, new and more expensive. That's what keeps the system alive. But it does mean that there will be rich and poor, exploiters and workers. Socialism on the other hand means that anyone can do any job that he wants, as long as he is qualified. Everyone is equal and everyone has what they need to live.)

Anyhow in 1968 the Russians invaded Czechoslovakia with Panzer tanks and troops in order to keep the old order in power in the country. People were killed and intellectuals fled, at least those that were able to flee. These are the sort of things that Igor knows and I feel fairly stupid next to him. But then I never feel particularly clever anyway.

I lie in bed and ask myself, what happens now. Igor's mother was quite appalled that Max simply went off. She's worried about him. She said that I should at least stay. And then Igor said, yes, please do. But he didn't sound exactly euphoric to me. Perhaps I'm only imagining things but he seems slightly less interested than he was before the whole kissing business. Anyway, that was yesterday. Now it's night, the moon is shining, and I have the most terrible feeling:

1. that I've made some sort of a mistake, and

2. that I belong NOWHERE.

When morning finally arrives I slip down the stairs. I mean has anyone ever wandered around a house that you don't know, that belongs to people that have nothing to do with you, having not slept all night? I can tell you it's a total misery.

Igor's mother has already gone to work. And Igor says goodbye as he rolls off to school. Just great! I'm hanging around the house like a grandfather. Or a grandmother. I can't just stay here until I'm eighteen. And wait for Igor to come back from school. And then later on, wait for him to come back from university. I HAVE to develop a life plan. But the idea makes me nervous because I really am still a child and I have no concept of the various different possibilities of making something of one's life.

I wander purposelessly around the strange house, make myself breakfast and then wash up, so I'm being useful. After that I lie on the sofa and read Igor's German books. In between I rummage through his personal things and find loads of letters in Czech that look as if they have come from girls; they've got little hearts on and things like that. Time passes not at all. After five hours I find it's only been ten minutes and I'm all hyped up. What will happen when Igor comes back from school? Will we have something to talk about? Or will we do a bit more kissing? Will he ask me to go out with him? Perhaps they'll set up a room for me here, I can learn Czech, attend school and we'll be a family. That's why I think about while I sit around the house with sweaty palms, and wait.

At some stage it begins to get dark outside and still no-one's back. So I take the spare key from the key rack and go outside. I can't bear all this sitting around any more. Humans are not made for that. Without thinking I walk down the main road and turn left into the wood, there's a mist rising over the pond and there's ... Igor, sitting in his chair, with a girl on his lap. At first I think that I've gone completely mad and that I'm looking at myself sitting on his lap. Then I realise it can't be me, because that girl has long black hair.

Okay, so that's how it is.

I stand there, my mouth open, possibly a bit of dribble coming out, and thoughts are just exploding in my brain. Or they're colliding with feelings. What an idiot! What a complete trolley! I can't stay here! Where do I go now! Max!!! How could I be such a treacherous cow! And who on earth is that pretty bint on his knee? Time to go!

I turn around and run. Run back into the house, pack my rucksack, steal some food from Igor's poor mother and write her a thank you note. Then I leave the house, the village, and feel slightly relieved. But I can't think about it now, about this feeling, because I have to concentrate on walking. I feel like a horse. My nostrils are flaring with rage as I stomp down the street and sweat. All I want to do now is go to Budapest. To Max. If he's still there, which might well not be the case. I wouldn't be there if I was him.

I am so furious with myself that all I can do is walk and I don't even notice the cold or the dark. I don't know if anyone from some future generation will be able to picture a country road in the East? Probably not. Or maybe I'm exaggerating the desolation of the surroundings and perhaps it looks like this outside all large cities, i.e. like there's nothing. Absolutely nothing.

A couple of pathetic Eastern bloc stars throw some light on my path. There's a bit of a wood to my left, a bit of a field to my right. The dire tarmac is full of holes. I'll have to take care, children are always disappearing into these huge holes. Far away I can see the feeble lights of farmhouses. There's not been a car for, I don't know, maybe an hour? At some stage it starts to get light. So I've been walking all night.

I hear the sounds of a machine in the distance. A tractor slowly approaches with loads of straw on the back. I pull myself up and put on my best hitchhiker's face: look lively, friendly and smile. The tractor stops and a nice old man waves to me. Perhaps he's a moose, I don't know. I climb onto the trailer and burrow into the straw and we head off at speed, at least thirty kilometres an hour. And in a funny sort of way I'm content.

I'm warm. I chew on a piece of cheese from Igor's mother and stare at the sky. Unfortunately the tractor stopped after an hour. The farmer had brought me as far as the highway. Bye-bye and he's off, leaving only silence behind. So there I am, on my own. With a signpost: Budapest, 300 kilometres. Three hundred. That's going to take some doing.

Max   I'm beginning to feel better.

After I've slept for about five hundred hours I go downstairs to the dining room. It is full of young people who all seem to be in a good mood. At any rate they're throwing bread rolls at each other like lunatics, as if they're shooting a scene from a film. It's well known that relaxed young people always throw bread rolls at each other in films. In real life however I find the whole thing less entertaining.

There are no proper bread rolls in the GDR. In the supermarket they just sell bits of rubber. There are a couple of bakers, I think there are two in our town, but if they're baking rolls on a Saturday you have to queue up for an hour and by the time it's your turn they've usually run out of the little buggers. Here, on the other hand, the bread rolls are thick and there is malted coffee, jam and cheese. Just like in the West, I think, although I've absolutely no idea if that's true.

The young people are all between about thirteen and twenty years old and bursting with get up and go. Everything in the room is wriggling and moving, everyone has so much energy. I find it quite spooky when everyone is bursting to get out and explore and experience and sing and dance. I think I'm more of the cultivated observer type.

There's a boy and a girl sitting opposite me, who I bet are around my age. Did I tell you that it's my birthday today? It's my first birthday on my own. Not that it makes a great deal of difference as my normal birthday goes something like this: my father clears his throat at breakfast, gives me ten marks and wishes me many happy returns. I don't think you can call that a party with swing.

The two opposite me are speaking in German. Of course I remain true to myself despite all my recent adventures. In other words, I'd never just start up a conversation with strangers. And I'm not all sure if I want to strike up a conversation with these two. Despite the delight at hearing my own language, there are limits. The girl looks exaggeratedly sexy, somehow dressed up. And the boy looks as if he worships her so much that he himself does not even exist.

The girl asks me, in German, if I would pass her the jam. I give it to her and the two of them start talking to me. Svea and Benni are apparently sister and brother (which I don't believe) and want to visit an uncle in Bulgaria (which I don't believe either). Svea is tall with dark hair, Benni is small, rotund and has red hair. The pair of them prattle on non-stop, a torrent of words that make me feel quite empty.

I don't know if I was ever the sort of un-complicated person who made friends easily. This is very normal behaviour with children: they stand like dodos next to each other and then in the blink of an eye they start playing with each other. All I can ever remember is being afraid of other children and never knowing how to take that first step. And it doesn't seem to have improved with age. It takes some time for me to relax with other people. Apart from Anna, that was different.

And so I think about Anna for the first time since yesterday. I am completely confused as to how I could have been so completely wrong about somebody. Everything about being with her felt just right. She must have noticed that too. I sense that I could start weeping on the spot. At the table surrounded by lovely compan-ions. No way, not going there. Quick distraction. Where had we got up to? Budapest. The sun is shining outside. There's a lot to see and I'm feel-ing as frisky as a foal.

On cue, the pseudo siblings ask if I want to do something with them. There are fantastic baths here. Baths? I ask you, I might not be a wimp but nevertheless I am still a boy, and it takes a lot of persuading to get a boy to a bath. But who cares, let's go and look at some baths. I have my swimming trunks with me because we were heading in the direction of Bulgaria.

This is what you call fate. To distract myself I hang out with two types I'd never normally pass the time of day with. I'm beginning to think that you can only really plan out your life to a certain extent. Bang and you've been run over by a bus. Or you're paralysed from the waist down because you got caught out by a virus. Or your mother dies. Not much planning to do there. The main thing is to survive.

We set off down the hill into the city and through the narrow streets. The people who live here must be so happy in their lovely little houses with views over this wonderful city. For just one moment it feels terrible not having a home. I long for a friendly family, for a nice blonde mother and a fat funny father. We would all live in just such a cosy house. And I could enjoy being young.

Instead I am meandering along with two complete strangers in winter, in a country that means nothing to me. And I enter some baths with ancient walls filled with warm damp clouds of steam. Fat white bodies are moving about in a pool. And we soon join them. Everything outside this water, which apparently is very healthy, is green. There are plaster mouldings and brilliantly-shining lights and everything seems very lordly, and possibly even ghostly through the steam. Perhaps we've landed in the underworld and the white bodies in the water are all dead. In which case we are either in heaven or in hell. It's not very clear which.

I did believe in God for a while and I was very happy with the whole thing. It was as if I had a father to talk to. But then I began to realise a bit more about the world and ... I mean, I don't want to appear a clever dick and maintain that I understood the world. No, I simply understood as much as you can as a nine-year old. There was the Vietnam War and all sorts of other things you just don't register as a child. But I had heard of the atom bomb. For a long time that was the thing that frightened me the most. We learnt that at some stage there would be a war between the USA and Russia as well as all those countries friendly to Russia. And we learnt what the atom bomb did: how people are irradiated and die. It was at that point that I decided God didn't exist. Because people are too evil. Well, capitalist people anyway. Now I'm a little older, I wish to remove that last reservation: I don't think that it makes any difference where people come from.

So I move about in the warm water. Now and then one of my white limbs comes to the surface, now and then a strange body touches mine. Like now. And the touching doesn't stop. Annoyed I turn around and look straight into Svea's eyes. She has got so close to me that I'm almost lying on top of her in the water. Not such a terrible situation for a boy, but there's something about Svea I just don't like, even though I can't say exactly what it is. So I laugh like an idiot and dive away.

Underwater I ask myself if she's trying to make a pass at me.

I find the whole thing extremely embarrassing.

Later on, as we're walking back through Budapest, Svea is giggling at me the whole time and snuggling up to me. Or am I just imagining it? No idea. But goes like this, every time: she giggles, and almost as if the giggling makes her reel and lose her balance, then she staggers – whoops – against me. And then she actually says 'Whoops!' and looks at me in a weird way.

When we're back in the youth hostel Svea asks me in the corridor: 'Shall we go back to your room for a bit of a lie-down?' I gather all my courage and say firmly, 'No!'

ANNA Did I ever tell you what a speedy hitchhiker I am?

After the tractor had put me down, it was only half an hour before I was picked up by a nice little car. Before I get in I suddenly have a moment of real panic. I mean, hello, I'm an under-age girl hitching on her own in a foreign country. But before my fear could really develop I noticed that there was an elderly couple sitting in the car, both of them about three hundred years old. The rest was just motorway.

And now it's evening. I'm standing on a bridge in Budapest and looking up at a castle on a hill. Well, don't hold me to that: it might even be a palace. In the East we got rid of the nobility and so we've got no idea what that sort of stuff is called. So there I am, standing and looking at those walls, the light is tinged with red from the disappearing sun and I think, I've simply got to run up there.

I like the city from the very first moment. There are places you just don't have to make an effort to like. I run through neat little streets in the direction of the nobles' hovel and stop for a short break in a café. I have to say that it is really sublime, to sit on your own in a café, to point at something on the counter that looks like the finest cake, and then be served like a fully paid up member of society.

I don't know if other children register the first time they do something and what it's like. And how you experience getting older. Sleeping away from home for the first time, going into a café on your own for the first time, kissing for the first time. This is a time of life that'll never come again, my mother once said to me. Later on everything is simply repetition and then life becomes so colourless. I think I can sort of understand. For example my very first Ragout Fin (for future generations: this is an Eastern bloc delicacy, finely-shredded chicken in a white sauce with melted cheese on top) was like an earthquake, although I've never actually experienced one. I got completely over-excited because of this wretched Ragout Fin and felt a maniacal desire to eat it again. I just can't describe the disappointment the second time round: I didn't feel anything. It was just something to eat. And that's what I think my mother meant. On the other hand I'm sure that adults have loads more opportunity to experience wonderful things — maybe even discover new nuances in Ragout Fin.

After the café I feel pretty fine and so

carry on up the hill. Right at the top, next to the castle or palace thing, there's a youth hostel. It's an ancient white house with a warm friendly light shining from it. Here we go with another first: I've never been alone in a youth hostel.

I did go to a youth hostel with the whole class once. In winter last year we went to Eisenach. At the top of a mountain there's a castle that you can ride right up to on a donkey. That was a real experience, not unlike riding a scooter. As a child you are very proud to have something to yourself that moves you around. Apart from that there was a lot of flirting between girls from my class and some boys from elsewhere. The sort of giggling in the corridor at night thing. Of course, no-one wanted to flirt with me, even though there was a boy I might have fancied. Like all the others, he fancied the beauty in our class, the one with the jeans and the hair. The school trip was no different to normal school: I was on my own following the others around, the girl I was sleeping above in the double bunk bed pulled a face at me, and in the dining room no-one made an effort to sit next to me. Nothing new there.

There is a fat old woman sitting at the reception desk of the youth hostel. She barely looks at me and assigns me a bed in a three-bed dorm. For fifteen marks. I walk up to the room with my bag. It's cold and much taller than it is wide. Right at the top in the middle is a light bulb. The three iron beds look very unused. There's a squeaky cupboard and a window in the wall. I like that. I sit on the window seat and look out over the city. The heating begins to work and I relax a bit.

This wonderful city is really far too colourful for the Eastern bloc. The houses are in better condition than ours, and I even saw corduroy trousers in the shops. I don't think I'm being pulled towards the capitalistic system but seeing so many goods in the shops just makes me feel joyful. It's not a matter of owning everything. Once you've carried the stuff home they lose half of the secret and appeal anyway.

After a while I get changed and walk adult-like into the city. While I'm wandering around the streets the thing I want most of all is a Walkman. I know that they exist in the West. I find it unbelievably exciting to be able to listen to great music while walking around. It's almost like being driven around in your bed. On your own island. Without music or someone walking alongside you simply feel vulnerable. And you feel watched.

It's quite cold and most of the people in Budapest are wearing fur coats. In the Eastern bloc many people wear fur coats, there's virtually nothing else to keep out the cold. The people have red, nice faces. Their language sounds as if they're singing. I walk around and nearly drown in all the shops. I have never seen anything like it. All of them are full of goods. And everything looks wonderful, whether it's food, clothes or books.

After a couple of hours I walk slowly back to the youth hostel. It's time for supper, included in the fifteen marks. The dining room is full to the rafters with loud young people. One boy is even playing a guitar. He reminds me of Igor, because he seems so self-confident and the girls are all worshipping him. Girls think that boys who play guitar are great. I've never understood it.

And then, suddenly, I see Max.

MAX   Anna is here.

She is standing in the queue for food and looking around the dining room. I'm sitting at the
table next to Svea and Benni. I look at her. She
looks at me. And without thinking I run over to
her. We embrace each other. We embrace each
other and hold on tight. I have never been so
happy in all my life.

It doesn't get uncomfortable for about
ten minutes.

Then it all comes back to me: she betrayed me! With that arrogant Igor! What is she
doing here? Is he here with her too? I release
myself from her grasp, and before I can say
anything, Anna says, 'Let's get out of here and
talk.' I'd already forgotten how well we understood each other.

I fetch my coat and follow Anna silently
through the little streets into a café. We sit
there like grown-ups. She doesn't say anything
for a long time. And then: how stupid she was,
that she had really fallen for Igor, that she is
ashamed of herself and that it was all a terrible

mistake. I am very quiet. It's quite obvious that I'm feeling very jealous. It's not a feeling I've felt very often, perhaps sometimes with my father, but in any case it's not very nice. When she admits to having real feelings for the prat, it's as if I've been ripped apart. I'm paralysed, I'm furious and I think: Aha, so I'm the jolly friend who's always meant to hold your hand when you're feeling lovesick.

I'm completely confused. I sit opposite Anna and am so happy that she's there. And I don't want her to go away. So I pretend to be strong and understanding. I am definitely in love with Anna.

Anna   Did I tell you about the next step of the journey?

The next morning we stand on the edge of the motorway like brave young things in hamster masks. Okay, the bit about the hamster masks is not true. Svea and Benni are with us. I don't really like either them but I don't say anything because I've got a bad conscience when it comes to Max. If he wants to carry on the journey with the two of them, then at this moment I'm in no position to protest.

We had a heart-to-heart. That's what the adults round us always say. In other words, I stammered a lot and Max didn't make a fuss. And after that it still wasn't all sorted. There's something there between us. But we're carrying on doggedly and trying to pretend that nothing has happened.

Waking up was good. The funny room was empty and I slouched along to the washroom where there was only ice-cold water. It burned on your body but then made you feel ridiculously euphoric. There were bread rolls for breakfast. I sat there and knew that I don't have to go back home and that we'd soon be by the sea. This is the first day of the rest of my life.

So now we're standing on the roadside going south. Svea is talking non-stop rubbish and throwing herself at Max. It's clear as a bell, women notice these things. First of all Svea sized me up from top to bottom, reckoned I wasn't much competition, and is now completely ignoring me. Benni is her stupid, fat hanger-on. If those two are brother and sister then I'm a film starlet. Svea's voice is just a bit too high and she's squeaking on the whole time talking complete nonsense. It goes something like this:

'I just love singing. The first time I got up on stage was the Christmas party at the place my mother works. I was six. I went down really well. On stage I feel completely at home. I've got three pairs of jeans. I've got just the right figure for them, which is why they look so good on me. Budapest is just great, it's like being in the West. I'm going to live in the West sometime, I'll be a singer. I think it's really important as a singer to be interested in everything. Don't you think so, Max? That's why I read so much. I read Zola when I was ten. And Heine. And Tucholsky. Politics is really important too. I quite like Karl Marx's theories, but my mother says they're impracticable. And I think it's great that so many things are happening right now. While we're on our travels. I mean, I'm young and something should always happen. Don't you think so Max?'

Yeah, yeah, I thought. And you can do origami and you've got a pony and that's precisely why you're standing here on the motorway in that stupid skirt. By the way, hitching as a foursome is a stupid idea. Who on earth has room for four people in their car? After a while the others begin to cotton on and so cunning Svea suggests that we divide into groups and meet on the Romanian border. Great idea, I think. Until she bravely squeaks on: 'So I suggest that we have a competition, Max and I will be in one group, Anna and Benni in the other, and whichever groups gets to the border first is the winner.' Then she grabs hold of Max and drags him after her. A couple of metres along the road she stops and waits for a car.

It's clear as daylight that we are the losers. Besides it pisses me off to see how she talks to Max. And what's worse, he didn't say to her: No, I want to be with Anna. But then I know I brought that on myself.

So I stand next to boring Benni and watch what the other two get up to. Svea has got into position, pulled up her skirt a bit and is pouting in a very odd way. Max is virtually hidden behind her. And surprise surprise, after five minutes a spritely-looking car actually stops and the pair of them are gone.

In silence I look at fat Benni. He is also one of those always left behind. After about half an hour I ask him if they're really siblings. His reaction is way over the top: he starts crying, everything about him is drooping, trembling and wobbling, and between sobs he manages to get out a couple of sentences.

Of course Svea is not his sister. But since Year One he has liked her, and about a week ago she told him that she wanted to hitch to Bulgaria. Benni was afraid and didn't want to go with her at all because he has nice parents and is a swot at school. Only I noticed that, he hasn't quite worked it out yet. Swots have a good time in school mainly because they don't notice that the others despise them. In any case, Benni set off with Svea because he has a crush on her. And now she's dropped him and he's afraid to go back. It's a pretty sorry mess he's in.

An hour later and we're sitting on the back of a lorry. The tarpaulin is rattling and the wind is blowing in. I've got nothing to say to sad Benni and enjoy the journey. At some stage everyone should have a go at riding in the back of a lorry, there's something about it.

For the first time in days I start to think about my mother. And I begin to feel downcast. Will she manage without me? But if I were to go back and look after her nothing would change. Nothing would change for her and nothing would change for me. I'd grow taller and stay sad. I'd be locked into that country forever and never see Amsterdam. Or Italy. I'd be like everyone else. I'd marry, probably a boy like Benni, have a child, get a flat, get divorced, go to work, and every morning in winter I'd drag myself down streets lined with smouldering dustbins.

That's how I imagine a future that I really don't want to be a part of. And all the time the lorry is rumbling us on in the direction of freedom and the stars and cold air blows in through the crackling tarpaulin.

MAX   Down in the dumps in Romania.

Svea did not shut up for one minute during the entire six-hour journey. I wonder if it really would be a crime to boot her out of the car.

A young man in sunglasses is at the steering wheel. At night! In the middle of winter! He's just the right type for Svea. She is flirting with him and talking at him non-stop. I've no idea if the guy understands a single word, but that doesn't seem to bother Svea. My only hope is that Anna is annoyed that I didn't defend myself when Svea grabbed hold of me. It was nothing but a cheap act of revenge. And now I have to pay the price.

Shortly before the Romanian border, the guy lets us out at a grim-looking bus stop. One thing at least, it does seem to be warmer here. Behind the bus stop is a block of flats. I have never ever seen anything so bleak – ever. Some of the windows don't have glass, and everything is so filthy and desolate that in comparison the GDR seems like paradise ...

Svea gets all het up because everything is so ugly and so cold. She wants to continue. But I've had enough and tell her that I'm waiting for Anna no matter what. Of course she could carry on alone if she wanted to. But she doesn't want to.

The bus shelter does have glass in it, although a couple of panes are all smashed in. There's a neon light hanging from the ceiling and all around the floor are cigarette butts. It stinks. On the other hand it's a couple of degrees warmer than outside. Besides, it's got benches. We get ready to do a fair bit of waiting and so cover ourselves with everything we have. Sadly we don't have any newspaper to put under us. One thing is for sure, I'm not going to be able to sleep properly.

Svea bangs on and on without taking breath. It's madness, this combination of energy and total lack of thought. How can you go on letting out such a stream of drivel for hours on end? Now she's talking about models and how she wants to be one. Yeah yeah.

At some stage Svea shuts up and falls asleep. When she's sleeping she looks really stupid. When people sleep they can't hide themselves. That's when you discover what they're really about. Some look very innocent. Others just look stupid.

I would advise every child to run away once. I think later on you just have too much to stop you from doing it. A library, decent co-workers, or a house and certain habits. Children don't really have that many habits. For example I'm not longing for my bed or for my room. They mean nothing to me. Or is that because I don't know how to value them?

I look around and ask myself — how can anyone live like this? In those pig-ugly houses. Don't people notice them? Why don't they just leave? Is there something I don't know about? Is there some sort of catch to running away?

ANNA   Did I ever tell you how we found each other again?

The man in the lorry was cool. He even offered us sandwiches. All in all a pleasant journey.

After about a hundred hours we crossed the border into Romania and virtually the first thing I see is Max, who is lying asleep next to Svea in a bus shelter smelling of piss. I'm so happy to see him that I run up to him and give him a kiss. Then things happen very fast.

Max wakes up, Svea wakes up and a police car stops. Half-drugged by the noise of the lorry and exhaustion I don't really get what happens. Suddenly we're all sitting in a police car. Svea is wailing, Benni is looking sadly and silently out of the window. Max is sitting next to me and holding my hand. Which is so nice that I really don't care about the rest.

The car stops in front of a sort of barracks. An extremely awful building with a sports ground in front of it that looks like the sort of place you put down dogs. We're shoved into the building, which is as shabby inside as it is outside and looks like a prison. And in a way it is a prison, at least that's what the badly-dressed woman with the bad German explains. We've landed in a home for runaway children. One ruled by discipline and order!

Then the woman doesn't say anything else. She pulls four sets of prison clothing, or something like that, out of a cupboard and then half dead, we drag ourselves after her into a washroom. Totally separated of course, one for boys and one for girls. There are stone troughs and the water is cold. Shaking, Svea and I get undressed and wash ourselves. It really is saying some, even Svea does it all without mouthing off even once.

I'm having real difficulty in taking the whole situation seriously. Maybe it happens to everyone when they come face to face with something dreadful: initially they don't realise what's going on. And when the brain has finally absorbed the shock, they've already got used to it in some way. I just really can't take all this seriously. And I've no idea what to file it under: children in an orphanage from the nineteenth century perhaps?

But if you think that my travels end here – then you'd be wrong.

After washing ourselves, we put on the scratchy uniforms; an old pair of trousers and a bleached out jacket, far too big and far too cold.

Finally the old woman pushes us down another corridor. Girls go into one dormitory, the boys into another. We are to make our beds and then eat. She says all this in Russian. That's what you call 'Understanding between Peoples'.

There are about a hundred beds in the dormitory, half of which are already made. I find a bed as far away from Svea as possible. I don't even bother to unpack my rucksack. The woman guarding us screams again that we should come out of there. At least I'm guessing that's what she's shouting, because right now my ability to take anything on board is very limited. You could even say that it's disappeared completely. So we go back out into the corridor. With a nod of her head the woman indicates that we should follow her. A revolting woman. Fat, with white hair that she's gathered into a small bun. She's got beard stubble on a chin that wobbles when she shouts. And she shouts all the time. I don't think she can talk normally at all.

We go into the dining room, which is about the most creepy place I've ever seen. There's no colour on the walls, there are small wooden stools and it smells foul. The woman gathers us around her. She says that first we'll get something to eat and then we'll go out to work with a young lad, who'll instruct us on what to do. This is followed by some nonsense like: here we will be brought up to be good citizens, laziness will not be tolerated, in fact it will result in corporal punishment. It's all completely incomprehensible. I mean, why don't they inform our parents? Or at least check our identity documents?

A greasy-looking boy of about our age comes out of the kitchen and places metal plates in front of us swimming with cold soup. I try one spoonful and want to choke, so I push the bowl to one side. Immediately the wardress is standing there next to me, ordering me to eat all the soup up. She terrified me so much that I manage to spoon every bit in. A tasteless cold broth with white, fatty meat swimming in it. Straight after I've gulped it all down, I have to run to the toilet to throw it back up. Things just couldn't get better, I feel.

When I come back, the others are all standing with the young greaseball ready for the off. None of us says a word. I think we're all in a state of shock and have to gather ourselves. We follow the boy silently out into the cold day and the ugly streets. We really do look pitiable in the tattered, thin clothes, our faces red with the cold. After a while the boy said that one of us should sit at the next corner. He presses a cardboard sign into Benni's hand along with a hat and tells us that he'll pick us all up in a couple of hours. All we have to do is beg for some money. If anyone doesn't collect enough, then they'll be beaten.

My head is still not very clear when I'm shown my place in front of a shabby department store. This is where I and my cardboard sign are meant to sit on the street. The whole thing is totally embarrassing. I barely dare look people in the eye. It's freezing cold. And the Romanians look pitiful. Rotten clothes and sad faces. And, of course, no money. Nobody gives me a thing.

After a while I forget everything, the home, the cold, the uncertainty and I sink into the moment. I look people in the eye, and this has an interesting effect. Those whose eye I manage to catch look away, embarrassed, then hunt around in their pockets and plop a coin into my hut. So that's how it works. I'd just love to know what it says on the sign. No doubt something about orphans.

After a while I begin to enjoy the whole thing. I make bets with myself as to who will give me something, and usually I'm right. It's easier to get money from women than it is from men, and in particular from older women. I don't feel the cold any more, no doubt my body has got used to shivering. So that's the trick, this is how people who are imprisoned survive, or maybe their best friend's died or their house has been annihilated by an earthquake. The brain is simply too slow to grasp the situation fully. So you just feel your way forward, to the next corner, the next meal. And if you think, then just think 'later on'. 'Later on' something will occur to me. The couple of wags we hold up as heroes, for example Störtebeker,* or Lenin or Marco Polo, they must have had some sort of a brain defect and that's why they were always able to deal with things without this helpful hesitation.

I sit there, stare ahead of me and think about irrelevant rubbish. At some stage the stream of people walking past slows down and the department store closes. Not long after that the others appear and we walk in silence to pick up Benni, who is sitting in a corner covered in tears. Svea on the other hand is blabbing away as usual, about how she wrapped the men around her little finger and how much money she made. Our watcher manages to shut her up with a couple of words. I walk next to Max. Maybe he's a hero.

* A former merchant who formed a pirate band called The Firends of God & Enemies of the World. They sailed the Baltic Sea and attacked the city of Bergen, in Norway. Störtebeker was caught and executed in 1402.

MAX   I gradually begin to wake up.

What on earth was all that about? The police, if they were police at all, the home, the begging business? Have I read too much Jack London? It's totally crazy what you can do with people. All you need is a uniform, act authoritarian, shout a bit and suddenly you can herd people about like sheep. Admittedly I've never herded sheep. Maybe that's more difficult.

    I never realised that that's how it all works. If you don't have a particularly strong sense of self, then you're putty in others' hands. People simply believe all those who act as if they're important: politicians, newspapers, policemen, lawyers. It's just a question of appearance. It's exactly the same with animals. Fluff up your hackles momentarily and hey presto you're top dog. I'm probably quite right to be afraid of people. Some people are stronger than others and take full advantage of the fact.

    Here I am making such wonderful speeches again. I am a born speech maker. Really. I'd look just right in a black tailcoat at Speaker's

Corner in Hyde Park. We heard all about it in one of our rare English lessons. A wonderful thing. Any madman can come along, stand there and talk. The end of the world is near and similar statements. But isn't it getting nearer all the time?

Our little troop of beggars arrives at the home just in time for supper. At least that's how it smells. But before we eat we have to see our overseer and hand over the loot. While we're doing just that, the room is filled with the sharp sound of a slap. And then another, right across Svea's face. Did she earn too little? Or maybe steal? The wardress rips the clothes off her body and sure enough, she has some coins in her pants. Man, how stupid can you get? Even so, it's not nice to watch the way Svea is being treated. It could happen to any of us. Well, to me and Anna. My solidarity with the others does have its limits.

So hiding cash is definitely not a good thing. The fat woman begins to hit Svea. And suddenly I see red. I jump on the wardress, bite her hand and hit at her madly, no idea where my fists are landing. She tries to shake me off and then suddenly Anna is hanging onto her. Together we make a fairly good hit squad. I'd never have thought it of us. In the middle of the rebellion we suddenly hear a whistle: Benni has grabbed hold of our clothes. I'd never have credited him with quite so much prudence. So we all storm out of the still-open door, Svea in her pants, and flee into the night.

No-one follows us. No dogs, no wardress. Just darkness. We put on our old clothes and run down the street in silence, in the direction of the city. I think that we're all rather embarrassed by the whole situation. Besides it's cold. Anna looks so pale that I notice it, even in the dark. I feel a bit hopeless.

Svea wants to go to the police straight-away. I think that's total madness, after all it was the police that took us to the home. She however thinks they were probably not real policemen. Benni goes along with her. Anna and I understand each other without have to utter a word. We have got to get out of this country.

So we accompany Svea and Benni until about half an hour later we arrive at the police station. It's an ugly barracks and looks like the sort of institute where they carry out experiments on humans. I hide with Anna in the dark so that we can watch how Svea and Benni are treated. Well, it doesn't go too well. After a couple of minutes the pair of them are pushed out of the station and loaded into a car. And the car sets off in a straight line back towards the children's home.

What a complete mess. But they only have themselves to blame. Which might sound un-friendly, but I really don't like them at all. Or is that too pathetic for words?

ANNA   Did I ever tell you that I'm a rescuer?

The only thing I want to do is wake up from this awful dream. Now Svea and that idiotic Benni are actually being returned to the revolting home. And tomorrow they will have to go begging again. You could call it socialist kitsch.

And however much I want to run away too, it's not possible. I can't bring myself to do it. Ten minutes later I've persuaded Max that we do have to help them. After all, stupid people are still people. So half dead with exhaustion we trot back down the horrible street to the home. I'm quite dizzy because I haven't eaten anything for twenty-four hours. And I really don't have to watch my weight.

When we first get to the home we've no idea how what to do. The door is locked, of course. And the dormitories are on the first floor. We wander around the desolate building lit up by a lone street lamp. And there, on the first floor, is an open window. Man, are they stupid or what? Now it's Max's turn, he is the man after all. He gets up on my shoulders, the way they do in films about gangs of thieves. I would like to be a gang of thieves right now, and eat boar on a spit. Although the poor little boar might have family ...

Max heaves himself up gingerly and goes through the window. All I have to do is wait and be afraid. I think it's much better to be the person doing the doing rather than the person doing the waiting and the not-doing.

Suddenly I realise how awful I feel. I'm ice-cold, dog-tired and so hungry that I'm almost not hungry any more. I stare at the window, which looks like an angry, blind eye. Man, Max, come on! My nerves are not up to being on my own just now. Or maybe not up to freeing all three of them. I want to go somewhere where it's warm as quickly as possible.

And then all at once: utter chaos!

MAX   Here we go.

I crawl through the window and into a broom cupboard. I open the door carefully and see the corridor ahead of me. This is where the girls' and boys' dormitories are. I know where Benni is sleeping, but I've no idea where Svea's bed is. I grope my way down the dark corridor and into the boys' dormitory. Benni is in the third row from the back. I hope he's not in solitary confinement or something like that. I knock into a bed, a boy grunts and I nearly have a heart attack. When I arrive at Benni's bed, I lean over him and whisper, 'Don't make a sound.'

Benni gets it straightaway and sits up. Somewhere a boy is muttering 'Quiet!' in Russian. A second heart attack. Benni staggers to his feet. I tell him to fetch his things and wait in the corridor. Then I slip over to the girls. This is not going to be easy.

A few stars light up the room. Sleeping girls look very similar to young sleeping bears, i.e. they're just black shapes. I creep about on all fours between the beds, because then I'm at about face level. One thing is sure: girls smell better than boys. I can't find Svea anywhere. Instead I find myself staring into the wide-open eyes of a girl who is definitely not Svea. She looks at me and starts to squeal. Within seconds all the girls are awake. So that's the second thing that's different to boys: it's impossible to wake up boys, even if you set a bomb off. I look around and finally spot Svea. She's not quite as dense as I thought either. She leaps out of her bed and runs after me into the corridor. Unfortunately without her things.

The three of us make it into the broom cupboard before a shrill alarm sounds. Benni is the first to thud out of the window, then Svea, finally I go. At least try to go. Because unfortunately the greasy lad, our begging-overseer, is hanging onto my leg. I manage to kick him away while I'm half hanging out of the window. And fall.

I can't put my foot down properly. Anna drags me behind a shed and from there behind a scrubby bush. The four of us sit there and watch the proceedings. The wardress and a large ugly man we haven't seen before stand under the lamp in front of the building. A minute later they split up and start hunting for us with torches. The only thing to do is hope and keep our mouths shut. Svea's in her nightie and my foot is kaput. This is going to be a barrel of laughs.

ANNA   Did I ever tell you that I'm Emil and the Detectives?

No, I'm not going to tell you that. But I thought it looked like a great title. The evil ones are swearing and running about with torches in the dark while we press ourselves into the half-frozen muddy grass and try not to breathe. I'm too exhausted to be afraid. It's all so ridiculous. Maybe I should just stay lying here and fall asleep. What a good idea. Suddenly the ground seems so friendly. And soft. I think of home, and it's cold there too. I'd like to be in a place that's warm. Like a cloud, that I could lie down on.

And suddenly I am Emil, I've got loads of friends, am super clever and everything is working out for the best.

MAX   Dammit.

The hunt is called off after thirty freezing minutes. I mean we're talking about four beggar
children — what's the problem. They've nothing
to fear from the police around here. Our little
group on the other hand is on its last legs. Svea
is crying, Benni is shaking. And Anna's fallen
asleep. Oh no, she can't fall asleep now.

And all at once I don't care about anything apart from Anna. I'm suddenly wide-awake.
'So, you two are on your own again,' I say to
Benni and Svea. And even if it isn't the ideal moment for such intimate confessions, I add: 'I don't
find you particularly inspiring.' They swallow, say
not a word, and leave. A good exit.

I grab hold of Anna and pull her to her
feet. She groans because she doesn't want to
wake up. I shake her, but it's like she's unconscious. So I drag her to the street. We've got to
get out of here. My foot doesn't hurt quite as
much but it's still not easy. What's more it's
night-time and every car could be a police car.
And then we're right back where we started.

What do I do? I'm pretty sure that even an adult would be strained by this situation. But the only thing I'm concerned about is how to get Anna better.

A lorry comes towards us. That's exactly what I need. With Anna in my arms I stagger in front of the lorry so that it has to break hard, and then yell loudly at the driver in Russian. 'We have to get out of here, we need a hotel quickly.' The man is a small grey thing and he looks shocked. Now he's got two shattered children in his lorry and has no idea what to do with them. He says he has to go to the sea. The sea is good! And then I fall asleep.

When I next wake up the lorry is standing in the sunshine and the sea is ten metres away. The man is sitting next to us. He didn't want to wake us. He's sitting there stiffly, he probably thinks we're aliens. I wake Anna. She's completely doolally and looks at me with blank eyes. She's not eaten anything for forty-eight hours and has been frozen the whole time. I have to warm her up. I help her out of the lorry. We are standing by the sea, on a beautiful promenade. I ask the man where we are, Constanza, he says. It sounds just great.

I haul myself and Anna to the nearest hotel. It's large and clean. I want a room for myself and the half-dead girl at my side. And that's precisely what I get. No idea how. Perhaps because I'm acting like someone who books a room in a hotel every day. I fill in the registration form, with great seriousness I compare the number of my child ID with the details I am writing down, and get a key. No shit! Every child should try this just once. Simply walk into a hotel and take a room. I mean, either I have seriously aged or they really have no idea at all.

We go up in the lift to our room on the sixth floor. I've never seen anything like it. It's huge and one wall is made of glass and behind the glass is a balcony that is in full sunlight. I tuck Anna into bed and order breakfast from room service. The whole time I'm acting as if I know exactly what I'm doing.

Fifteen minutes later there is a knock at the door and no, it is not the police, but a girl about our age with a trolley. On it are scrambled eggs, rolls, juice, tea and jam. I am so overcome by how relaxed I am that I nearly do a double take.

ANNA   Did I ever tell you how I woke up in paradise?

It smells of food. I open my eyes and I'm lying on a soft bed. There's breakfast on a trolley. Behind the trolley is a balcony and behind the balcony is the sea. I have no idea how or why.

Got to eat first. Fresh rolls with scrambled eggs and tea. I eat for about four hours. Then I stand up and wander around the room. How on earth did Max do it? Then I'm standing in a warm bathroom and it's true, hot water really does come out of the tap. I fill the bathtub and could squeal with pleasure. So I do squeal with pleasure. Tiny little squeals, the sort piglets probably make.

I lie in the bathtub for an hour. Then I soak all my clothes because they're filthy and smell foul. While they're soaking I lie back down on the bed. And fall straight back to sleep.

When I wake up again it's already midday. The washing is hanging up on the balcony. And Max is sitting next to me and looking at me. I am so happy.

MAX   I think I'd better go and have a bath.

Even though I'm a boy, I think I'd better go and have a bath. I've already washed my stuff. I have to confess that I'm a bit all over the place.

I was so happy that Anna was fed, clean, warm and washed. As she woke up I just wanted to hug her and hold her tight. But I'm not so sure.

So, as I said, I thought I'd better go and have a bath. When I came out of the bathroom Anna was sitting on the balcony and looking out at the sea. It's very hot in the sun but you can't go swimming even so. Instead we'll go and look round the town and pretend we're on holiday. I must admit I'm slightly scared that at some stage the police are going to come after us. Because it just can't be the right thing for us to book a hotel room like adults. But hey!

I get changed. I still have a clean pair of trousers and a pullover. Anna is ready to go. Then we walk down the steps coolly, nod to the woman at the reception desk and walk out onto the street. It's only a couple of minutes into the town. Really it is one of the most beautiful places I have ever seen, with magnificent houses, little restaurants and rampant plants. There are even palm trees dotted about. I have never seen a real palm tree in my life. Then of course there are souvenir shops. Everything is so strange and so beautiful. The air is warm and we wander through every single little street. Many of the little houses have rooms to rent. That might be better than a hotel. Living here in a little room. With Anna.

ANNA   Did I ever tell you how I just forget everything?

I just don't know how it happened. All at once I'm walking through the small town holding hands with Max. The walking part is not exactly exciting. I mean people do just wander around small towns. Even though I have to say it's particularly beautiful here. But holding hands. The last time I did that was with my mother about two years ago.

There was something was not quite right about holding hands then. But now it seems just perfect. Nothing is slipping or sweating. Our hands seemed made for each other. And at the same time it's very exciting. Like being adult.

And for the first time we're not on an adventure, we are on holiday. As if my mother and Max's father had turned into our parents and were sitting in the lovely hotel and stroking each other's hands. And we are brother and sister or something like that and have pocket money to spend. Later on we'll go out to eat with our fantastic parents. And it's just the beginning, the beginning of a two-week holiday.

I turn into a real girl and drag Max into one shop after another. I try on a folkloric blouse in one shop. They used to sell them in the GDR in boutiques. Everyone wanted to get their hands on one. They are white and have puffed-up little sleeves and are embroidered. I look fairly ridiculous in it. Like some amateur actress at a country show. Max is so touched by my hideousness that he buys me one. And then it's onto another shop that sells jeans. No, that was a joke. You can't get jeans here either. We buy ice cream, wander around and talk very little. We're excited and somehow keyed up at the same time. I want to buy everything. Everything looks just great. The town, the shops, the blouse. As if there is no reality; no aliens, no farm-workers' co-operatives.

I think this is it. I think this is happiness.

MAX   How quickly the mood can change.

We walked around the town all day. At some stage I took hold of Anna's hand. This is the second time in my life I do this. I already told you how the experiment with my father panned out. Anna didn't pull away. Nor she did look at me quizzically. It feels just right. For a couple of hours I feel like a hero.

It's getting colder. We've been into every shop and tried every flavour of ice cream. Now I'm shivering. It's because the damn day is nearly over. And the shivering makes me afraid. Out of nowhere it occurs to me that we are nothing. We're not adults, nor are we the children of someone we like. Nor can we stay here forever. We have to get away. By boat.

And as if our legs had worked that one out already, we end up in the port. A huge port. With freighters, cranes and all that. And just then, as the sun goes down and my stomach is full, I suddenly lose all courage. For the first time.

I'm afraid.

ANNA   Did I ever tell you how we suddenly got afraid?

While we're in the port our mood suddenly plummets. Man that was quick. Suddenly I couldn't think of anything to say. So the first thing we do is go into a restaurant. We sit there and there's a dead fish in front of us that takes a bow and begins to tap. No, that's not what I wanted to say.

So there we are sitting there. It's already dark outside because it's still winter. It's cooled down as well. And we no longer feel so strong or even grown up. We're silly children who ran away, and now we have to keep on running further and further away, through foreign countries and foul children's homes. We might even have to think about stealing at some point. I've no desire to think about that just now.

Slowly and carefully we start to talk to each other. We've got to find out what the situation is.

MAX   The situation is this:

We have parents who don't really like us. Or if they do like us, they can't show it. Which is the same thing in the end. The country that we call home is like a prison and we can only really look forward to a moderately interesting future. We probably can't become what we want to become, should we ever find out what that might be, because we have to become what the State wants us to become. And what's more, we don't have any friends.

That is what we've left behind.

ANNA   Did I ever tell you how courageous we were and decided to carry on?

I reply to Max: so we have to be courageous and carry on. We have to pretend to be more courageous that we really are; in some countries we'd already be married. Or had to go out to work. So let's not be afraid. And then let's think about what it will be like when we are free.

MAX   How I envisage freedom.

Let's say that we end up in Turkey, for example. Although we might not want to stay in a country where everyone wears a folkloric blouse and has a moustache, even the women. Not that I have the slightest clue what Turkey might actually be like, but it simply doesn't sound like our final destination. We'll find a friendly lorry driver who'll take us to Holland. He's bound to have cheese and tulips to pick up. We'll spend a couple of nights on a park bench in Amsterdam, and we are talking about an extremely comfortable park bench, and then find an apartment in a Kracht house. 'With a view over the Kracht canal?' Anna asks. 'With a view over the Kracht,' I say, 'and there'll be small bridges and bicycles. There'll be a lot of velvet in the flat. Maybe we'll help with the tulip harvest, eat lots of simple, hearty cheese and develop our capabilities. Later on we'll probably both have important careers. You'll write poems and I'll …' and I couldn't think of what I'd do, so I stopped talking.

ANNA   Did I ever tell you how I imagine the future?

Max has his own ideas about the future, and they're not to be sniffed at. I'm touched by the fact that he suddenly sees our life happening in Holland. His dream was always to go to Italy. Boys do tend to dream while girls are more pragmatic. One of my favourite words, pragmatic. It means – not getting lost in nonsense. I'm not sure that the Dutch are likely to let us rent an apartment with a view of the Kracht. It's more likely that we'll be sent to a Dutch boarding school, where we'll receive a wonderful and humanistic education. We'll be eighteen in a few years and then we'll study. We'll have a small student flat and I think it's always warm in Amsterdam. I once saw a book about the city in the library. It was sunny and there were cafés everywhere. Did I already mention that we don't have cafés? Nothing where there are chairs outside and young people, instead we have dives for old people with cheesecake that tastes like rubber, not that I've eaten a lot of rubber, but something similar. And grey people sit around with plastic tablecloths and shovel the stuff down. Where was I? I think growing up happens pretty fast, if you consider that last year alone I grew by ten centimetres. I'm quite clear that I'll stay with Max. Later on we'll have a house to ourselves, with sunny rooms, and we'll do grown-up things. But I don't tell Max that. Boys quickly lose the will to live if everything doesn't happen straight away. And the last thing we need right now is glumness. So I say, 'That's what it'll be like in Amsterdam. You'll see, tomorrow we'll be off on a ship and we'll look out through the porthole, and I swear to you a seagull will fly past as a sign that everything is going to be exactly what we wished for.'

Then I don't say anything else. Max doesn't say anything either. And the dead fish stays ominously quiet. Suddenly Max takes my hands. Just like in films, I think. But I'm a tiny bit shocked. Then Max says: 'We'll do it.'

At first it's quite embarrassing and then I notice how nice it is when someone holds your hands. I look Max in the eyes and my stomach is all fluttery. And so that my thoughts don't wander anywhere else, I add quickly: 'Yes, we'll manage.'

On the way back to the hotel we go past the port one more time. It's called confrontation therapy. Like stroking snakes because you're terrified of them. We creep through the wire fence and there we are, standing within the port perimeter next to all the huge freighters and cranes. A couple of workers walk past but don't seem to find it curious that two children are hanging around. Max is pushing, he wants to go back to the hotel. And I'm pushing, I want to look at the ships.

A huge ship is moored up at the end of the harbour basin. It looks like a giant steamer and has a Turkish flag. I feel all queasy. That is our ship. Now all we have to do is keep a clear head. The ship bobs happily away and makes no sign it is going to start the engine. Perhaps it's leaving tomorrow? No idea, but whatever happens now it's time to act.

'Let's go,' I say, 'we'll collect our belongings and leave. For good.'

MAX   I'm petrified.

I walk behind Anna as if I'm drugged. She is
so decided. Which is very good because at this
moment I've no idea what I want.

We walk back into the hotel and up to
our room. Anna puts on as many clothes as possible and advises me to do the same, because it
will be nippy out at sea. How on earth does she
know that? I put on as many clothes as possible
anyway and fetch the drying clothes from the
balcony and put them in our rucksacks. Anna
tells me to go downstairs and stand under the
window. A few minutes later I'm standing down
there in the darkness. Anna waves from the balcony, then she throws our rucksacks down. It
seems an age before she comes down herself.
But there's a good reason: she's got a large
bag with food and mineral water for the crossing
that she ordered from room service. Very clever.

Then it's off to the harbour. I don't know
how Anna's feeling because we don't talk. Occasionally we whisper something as if someone
could hear us. We creep back through the hole

in the wire. It all seems so unreal. Are we really going away? For ever? To the heart of capitalism? And will I ever see my father again? Because one thing is clear, if we do succeed in fleeing, then we will never be allowed back. We will be enemies of the state.

The Turkish ship is there. At least, I really hope it's from Turkey and not from Russia. That'd be great, to wake up after a great long journey and be in Nowosibirsk. We hide behind a container because the ship is being guarded by a man with a weapon, who is keeping an eye on the port. Perfect.

'Ready,' says Anna, 'an old spy trick.' And she throws a stone at a container a long way away. The man flinches and heads off in the direction of the noise. 'Now,' Anna murmurs. She got the murmuring from a film too, I'm sure. We run over to the ship, ducking down low, then up the steps and actually make it on board. And that's where we're standing now. What next?

I've no idea where's a good place to hide. Definitely not in the lifeboat. They're situated outside on deck and at sea it can get nippy. We open a metal door and climb down some steep steps into the bowels of the boat. Here we find a storage room that is far too visible, an empty swimming pool and finally a laundry room. It's perfect. It's warm and not easy to oversee, and on the shelves are mountains of clean washing. This is the place. Carefully we close the door behind us and find a comfortable spot in the middle of the clean sheets. Anna turns off the light.

And as we lie there I notice that I feel completely empty, in my head, in my stomach, no idea where. I feel like a nervous piece of meat.

ANNA   Did I ever tell you how simple it all was?

We lie in the laundry room of this (hopefully) Turkish ship. It has a porthole and is nicely messy. By the time someone finds us here we'll be well away. The Black Sea is not so huge after all. It doesn't take longer than a week to get anywhere.

Max is afraid. But I'm not worried. He's a boy, they're always more afraid about things that are really important. They're great at getting rid of spiders, but I'm not so sure about earthquakes.

About an hour later a rumble goes through the ship. It's a monster noise. It's sounds as if huge pistons are beginning to work. And that must be what is happening. I think we're putting out to sea.

I hold Max's hand. We lie on the white bed linen and look through the little porthole at the sky. Then we look at each other and I give him a kiss. We hold onto each other tight and look out of the stupid little porthole and I think: it was worthwhile being brave. It doesn't matter what happens next, it will be better than what we left behind. It will be something new. And of course at that moment a seagull flies past the window.

HOTEL**santo.**

X L Y   MOVING CLOSER

X L Y   IT'S HUMAN NATURE

LET'S GET TOGETHER

LET'S GET TOGETHER

LET'S GET TO GETHER

LETS GET TOGETHER

LET'S GET TOOETHER

LET'S GET TOGETHER **RIGHT** NOW!

Editor
RAPHAEL GYGAX

Translator
PENNY BLACK

Copy-Editing
CLARE MANCHESTER

Design
GAVILLET & RUST

Typeface
HERMES-SANS (www.optimo.ch)

Cover
RITA ACKERMANN

All images courtesy
RITA ACKERMANN (cover, p. 16, 107,
133, 188, 218, 237); ANDRO WEKUA
(p. 26, 74, 123, 151, 156, 205)

Rita Ackermann is represented by
the Galerie Peter Kilchmann, Zurich,
the Galerie Almine Rech, Paris and
Andrea Rosen Gallery, New York.

Andro Wekua is represented by the
Galerie Peter Kilchmann, Zurich
and Barbara Gladstone Gallery,
New York.

Production
CHE HUBER, Noir sur Noir, Geneva

ISBN 978-3-905770-77-3

© 2007, Sibylle Berg, Rita Ackermann,
Andro Wekua, JRP|Ringier
Kunstverlag AG

All rights reserved.

To know more about our program
visit our website:
www.jrp-ringier.com.

JRP|RINGIER
Letzigraben 134
CH-8047 Zurich
Switzerland
T +41 (0)43 311 27 50
F +41 (0)43 311 27 51
E info@jrp-ringier.com